The Sisters Club

W9-BWQ-365

So The Sisters Club

MEGAN McDONALD

SCHOLASTIC INC.
New York Toronto London Auckland Sydney
Mexico City New Delhi Hong Kong Buenos Aires

This is a work of fiction. Names, characters, places, and incidents are either
products of the author's imagination or, if real, are used fictitiously.

No part of this publication may be reproduced, stored in a retrieval system,
or transmitted in any form or by any means, electronic, mechanical, photocopying,
recording, or otherwise, without written permission of the publisher. For information
regarding permission, write to Candlewick Press, 99 Dover Street, Somerville, MA 02144.

ISBN-13: 978-0-545-14718-7
ISBN-10: 0-545-14718-2

Copyright © 2003, 2008 by Megan McDonald.
Illustrations copyright © 2008 by Pamela A. Consolazio. All rights reserved.
Published by Scholastic Inc., 557 Broadway, New York, NY 10012,
by arrangement with Candlewick Press. SCHOLASTIC and
associated logos are trademarks and/or registered trademarks of Scholastic Inc.

12 11 10 9 8 7 6 5 4 3 2   9 10 11 12 13 14/0

Printed in the U.S.A.   40

First Scholastic printing, January 2009

This book was typeset in Cheltenham, Kidprint, and Passport.

"This Is Just to Say" by William Carlos Williams, from
Collected Poems: 1909–1939, Volume 1, copyright 1938
by New Directions Publishing Corp. Reprinted by permission of
New Directions Publishing Corp.

"My Love" by Tony Hatch © 1966 by Welbeck Music Ltd.
All rights administered by Songs of Universal, Inc. (BMI).
Used by permission. All rights reserved.

Special thanks to Eliza Broaddus for the poem "I'm Sorry" on page 71

Lexile is a registered trademark of MetaMetrics, Inc.

For my sisters:
Susan, Deborah, Michele, and Melissa

The Middle

Being in the middle is like being invisible. Especially when you're the middle sister in a family with three girls.

Think about it. The middle of a story is not the beginning or the end. The middle of a train is not the caboose or the engine.

The middle of a play is intermission. The middle of Monkey in the Middle is a monkey. The middle of Neapolitan ice cream is . . . vanilla.

"I'm vanilla!" I shouted one day to anybody who would listen. Plain old boring vanilla.

Nobody listened.

Alex, my older sister, ignored me. She just kept writing stuff in the margins of her play script (what

1

else is new!) and muttering the lines under her breath.

Easy for her. She's strawberry.

I was sick of it, so I told my family how I hate being the middle. Middle, middle, middle.

"Hey! The middle of 'Farmer in the Dell' is the cheese!" Joey, my younger sister, reminded me.

"The cheese stands alone," I reminded her back.

Alex looked up. "There's a book about that, you know. *I Am the Cheese.*"

Yeah. My autobiography, I thought.

"Wait. You think you're cheese or something?" Joey asked.

I ignored her. They just don't get it. I mean, the middle of a year is, what, Flag Day? The middle of a life is a midlife crisis!

I told my dad I was having a midlife crisis.

"You're going to give *me* a midlife crisis if you don't get over this," Dad said. I asked him to name one middle that is a good thing.

Dad had to think. He thought and thought and didn't say anything. Then finally he told me, "The middle of an apple is the core."

"Um-hmm. The yucky part people throw away," I said.

"How about the middle of the night? That's an interesting time, when people see things differently."

I pointed out that most people sleep through the middle of the night.

Then he shouted like he had a super-brainy Einstein idea. "The middle of an Oreo cookie is the sweet, creamy, best part. You can't argue with that."

He was right. I couldn't argue. If I had to be a middle, that's the best middle to be.

"See? You're the peanut butter in the sandwich," said Dad. "You're the creamy center of the cookie that holds it all together. You're the glue."

I'm the glue?

Maybe Dad's right. After all, I'm the one who came up with the (brilliant!) idea for the Sisters Club, back when I was Joey's age. Alex gets to be the Boss Queen, of course, so she runs the meetings. Joey (a.k.a. Madam Secretary/Treasurer) takes the notes and collects dues (if we had any money). I keep the peace.

I am the glue!

The Sisters Club Charter
by Joey Reel

Alex is the sock monkey freak. Personally I find them a little... creepy. ~S

CLUBHOUSE: Alex's room

Unless sign on door says KEEP OUT! Joey + Stevie that means you! A.

MEMBERS: Reel sisters only

No fair! She gets the cool room with a window seat. ~S

UNIFORM: Pj's are good. Plaid is bad.
   Except when it's pj's.   (According to Fashion Queen Alex.) ~S

MASCOT: Alex's sock monkey, named Sock Monkey
   (I wish it was Hedgie, my hedgehog.)

LOGO: Three sock monkeys arm in arm

ALTERNATE LOGO: Troll doll with the "no" sign over it

SECRET SIGN OR HANDSHAKE:
   Hook pinkies together while saying,
   "Sisters, Blisters, and Tongue Twisters."

This is so lame! A.
You made it up. ~S
Yeah, when I was like ten. A.
Hello! That was only two years ago. My age! ~S

SECRET KNOCK: I don't know how to write it!
I just know how to do it. Sounds like:
Da-da-da, da-dee-dee-doh.

← I take credit for thinking of this.... That's why it's cool! A.

PASSWORD: Shakespeare (Shh! Don't tell!)

ACTIVITIES: Tell secrets and scary stories,
eat popcorn and ice cream,
stay up late,
have sleepovers in Alex's room
(I mean the clubhouse!).

DUES: Only if we need popcorn or ice cream and
we're out of them. yeah, right! Alex NEVER has money. ~S

RULES: No throwing pillows or other objects,
except in an official pillow fight.
No putting crumbs in Alex's bed on purpose.
No using Alex's brush to brush your hair
No taking stuff from Alex's room
(especially anything with glitter).

Or Hedgie the Hedgehog's hair. A.

Nut Jobs!

"No saying 'nut job'" is Alex's latest rule, which Joey has added to the list. Of course Joey had to ask, "What's a nut job?"

"It's a peanut who's looking for work," Alex said. The two of us cracked up.

"OK, I have a rule," said Joey. "No doing that."

"What?"

"That thing where you don't answer a question right. Then you laugh and act like I'm a nut job."

"No saying 'nut job'!" screamed Alex.

All three of us piled on the bed, laughing our heads off.

"But can we at least say 'nut' *or* 'job,' even if we don't say them together?"

"NO!" screamed Alex again. "Because that would make you a nut job."

We died laughing some more, which Joey says is the best part of the Sisters Club.

For me, the best part has always been the Remembering Game. And Alex is the best at it.

MARSHMALLOW TOES
Starring Alex

SETTING: SISTERS CLUB MEETING
PLAYERS: THREE SISTERS

Joey: Sisters, Blisters, and Tongue Twisters. Let's play the Remembering Game!

Me: Do you both solemnly swear not to repeat anything you're about to hear?

Stevie and Joey: We do!

Me: OK. Everybody pull up a pillow. *(We all lie on pillows and stare up at the ceiling.)*

Joey: Tell one about me!

Me: Joey, remember when you were an eggplant in the Thanksgiving play in kindergarten?

Joey: Yeah! Matthew Martinez said I had to go stand in the corner all by myself because there were no eggplants at Thanksgiving dinner, and I started to cry.

Me: And all your purple face paint got washed away.

Stevie: And you tried to convince everyone you were a giant grape!

Joey: That kid's in my same class in third grade and he *still* calls me Eggplant.

Stevie: No way!

Me: Stevie, remember that time you wore your pajamas to school by mistake?

Stevie: It was pajama day!

Me: Was not! OK, then, remember when you stole that blue marble from the Ben Franklin store, and . . .

Joey: *What?* You *stole*?

Me: Don't worry. Stevie felt so bad, she went and turned herself in. All they did was make her put it back.

Stevie: OK. My turn. Remember when Joey begged Mom and Dad to see the elephants at the zoo, and then as soon as she saw them, she *threw up*?

Me: That's the best!

Joey: How come all the throwing-up stories are about me?

Me: They just are. We never throw up. OK, I have one about me. How about the time I convinced you to put marshmallows between your toes?

Joey: I don't remember *that.*

Stevie: Me neither.

Me: Good. Because we haven't done it yet. We're going to do it right now.

Stevie: No way am I putting marshmallows in my toes.

Joey: Toe jam!

Me: It's a Health and Beauty Tip. I read it in a magazine. Put marshmallows between your toes, and it makes it easier to paint your toenails.

Joey: Glitter toenails—cool!

Stevie: Like I really care about toenails. And just one time I'd like to see one of these famous magazine articles you're always quoting. Like how to eat pizza without smearing your lip gloss.

Me: Check my locker. They're there.

Stevie: You just say it's in a magazine to make it sound important.

Joey: C'mon, Stevie. It sounds like fun. And we can remember it later.

Stevie: What about the Sisters Club?

Marshmallow feet are not in the charter.
There are rules.

Me: New rule. Joey, write this down. "All members
of the Sisters Club must try putting
marshmallows between their toes if they
want to be in the club."

Joey's Homework Notebook

This is my notebook. It looks like a real one for school. You know, the black-and-white kind that makes your eyes go cuckoo when you stare at it? Actually, I pretend it's a diary, because both of my big sisters, Alex and Stevie, think diaries (especially locked ones!) are way cool.

Hey, I just thought of one thing they agree on!

But really, this is going to be my Homework Notebook. My big sisters think I'm nuts (not a nut job!). (The #2 thing they agree on!) They hate homework. But, I mean, by third grade, shouldn't a person be old enough to get homework?

All we get are worksheets.

Baby stuff.

So . . . I like to make up homework for myself.

My little sister, the homework freak. ~S

Story of My Life
by Joey Reel

My (made-up) homework today is to write about me. Stevie says that's an autobiography. I had to help her spell that, too. ~S

Hi. My name is Joey. Not Joan. Not Jo-Ann or Josephine or Jolene. Not Jo-Anything.

Whatever. –J

Just Joey.

How about Jethro? A.

Good one!
~S

I guess it's better than Jeremy. Or Jerome.

Mom and Dad named us all for boys. For some strange reason, they could only think of good boy names when we were born.

Stevie says Dad wanted a boy. Mom says all three times she was sure she was having a boy. When it got to me, she was really, really, really sure, 'cause boys kick a lot or something.

Even the doctor yelled, "It's a boy!" when I first came out.

But it wasn't a boy! It was me, Joey. And I don't kick, even though Stevie says I do— like when we have sleepovers in Alex's room. But who wouldn't kick inside a sleeping bag!

Ha!
Try sleeping next to you. You play soccer in your sleep. ~S

My big sisters call me Duck. See, when I was little, I called everybody (Stevie and Alex) and everything "duck."

Most times I hate being called Duck. It's not like I have two almost-webbed toes (like Stevie!) or anything.

It just makes me feel like a baby.

Hey, no making fun of my two webbed toes— they're unique! ~S

yes,— I'm not a baby. Yes, you are! A.

yes, you are! ~S

I read chapter books!

Dear Sock Monkey:
My sisters call me Duck. It makes me feel like a baby, but I'm not a baby anymore!! Help!!
—Quackin' Mad (a.k.a. Joey)

Dear Quackin':
Make sure you show them you're not a baby, and they'll stop treating you like one. If that doesn't work, try calling them Quack and Moo!
∗ Sock Monkey ∗

OUR TOWN
Starring Alex

I come from a family of actors. Not just Mom and Dad, but a long line.

I love, love, love living in Acton, because we have a one-hundred-year-old theater and this town has had plays 4-ever (as Joey would say).

It all started with our great-great-grandmother, Hepzibiah McNutty Reel. Yep, that's her name, for real. My dad has the family tree to prove it.

When I star in a play, people say, "That's Hezzy's girl," like she's my real-life grandma living down the street or something, even though she'd be like a million years old.

Stevie says how can I be happy about being descended from anybody with the name Hepzibiah? She thinks our whole family is Mc-Nutty!

I think old Hezzy is cool. They say she rode a horse for thirteen hours through so much snow that her feet froze right to the stirrups. Bugs and bears and stuff didn't stop her. Not one bit. But the coolest thing? She wore bloomers so she could look like a lady but ride horses like a man.

Hey, maybe that's where I get my fashion sense.

Acton wasn't anything but a wide spot in the road back then, so Hezzy put on plays at the old Raven Theater just to give people around here something to do.

Mom wants a *real* house someday, which means a *new* one. But this house has *history*. I mean, Hezzy's ghost could be hanging around in the rafters with the spiderwebs, watching over me. I like thinking Hezzy might have looked out the same window I do, practicing lines for a play.

How could I not love acting, right? As Dad says, "You're a Reel. It's in the blood."

Pioneers Rock!
by Joey Reel

The best thing about our town is the Rock, right in the middle of the town square. Dad says it sounds like a jail. Alex says it sounds like a funny nickname for an actor. Mom says it sounds like a big fat diamond ring.

Stevie says it sounds like a rock.

It is! A real rock. Made out of . . . rock!

I call it Pioneer Rock. It's been there forever, since olden days. The pioneers carved their names there. You can still see HEPZIBIAH MCNUTTY on it if you know where to look.

I traced over it gazillions of times. Some rubbings I made are hanging all over one wall of our room.

Stevie says you can almost hear the wagons creaking and squeaking down the ruts in the road. I think she's just saying that to tease me, but for real you can almost hear them.

If you close your eyes.

They paint the rock now. To tell you when there's a concert or dance, or a play, or a puppet show at the library. Hello! They should not, I repeat, NOT paint over pioneer names. Pioneers rule!

Mom made a pioneer costume when Alex was little, and she passed it down to Stevie, and Stevie passed it down to me. It has a calico dress and apron and a big bonnet and killer button-up shoes. I can't wait to wear it for Pioneer Day at school.

Alex and Stevie say it makes me look like a geek. But I think I look like LIW (Laura Ingalls Wilder), and LIW was not a geek! They didn't even HAVE geeks back then.

For Pioneer Day, we get to dry up old apples and make dolls out of them and learn how to churn butter.

Note to self: Save old apples.

King Lear

My whole family is crazy about acting, but I hate standing up in front of an audience. I once told my dad I was missing the Reel acting gene.

"Hogwash!" (He actually said that.) "Everybody likes a good story. Just because you don't want to perform in front of people, like Alex, doesn't mean you don't have an actor in you." Dad says, "All the world's a stage, even the living room!"

He's the set builder for the Raven, so he's always making stuff for this play or that. We've had dinner with the Mad Hatter, a giant Nutcracker, and Santa's reindeer (all eight). Our dining room has been an underground rabbit hole, a Kansas tornado, a Civil

War battlefield, a fire station, and a medieval castle where you have to cross a moat just to eat at the table.

And he lets us put on *King Lear* in our own living room anytime we want.

That's why *King Lear* is the only play I like.

King Lear is Dad's favorite play, too. I wonder why. It's about this guy who has three daughters! They have weird names.

If you think Stevie's a funny name for a girl, try Goneril, Regan, or Cordelia. Cordelia's not so bad. (That's Joey, the youngest, and the good one—King Lear's favorite. Joey never lets me be Cordelia. Not once!) At least Cordelia sounds like a flower. Not a president or a yucky worm.

Each daughter tells him how much they love him so they can get his kingdom, but the older ones are just faking. Really they're super-greedy. They each keep pretending the other one is trying to murder King Lear, and they try to poison each other (YES!). People get stabbed (with a dagger) and eyeballs come out (POP!).

So King Lear goes outside and yells at a thunderstorm (a.k.a. cookie sheet!).

He gets to say lots of funny-sounding words like "Alack" and "O nuncle!" and stuff.

The play is a tragedy. It's supposed to make you cry, but it doesn't. It usually makes us laugh our heads off. (No heads really come off—just eyeballs!) Or we end up in a fight. King Lear (Dad) usually lets Cordelia live and get the kingdom, which makes Alex and me mad. Then we say, "How come Joey always gets her way?" (So true, even though Joey says it's so NOT true.) Then Alex quits, then I quit, and Joey yells, "The end!"

King Lear Props
by Joey, Supreme Note-Taker, List-Maker

- Map of England (You can write on cloth if you want.)
- Jester hat (with *bells*!)
- Plastic dagger
- Eyeballs! (One guy gets his eyes poked out—gross!)
- Cookie sheet (Stevie's idea—for making thunderstorm noises!)

Favorite parts from King Lear:
- "Out, vile jelly!" (Stevie says, "Out, vile Jell-O!")
- "You stinkard!" (I.e., stinkhead)
- "Off with his head!" (We say this even if it's not in the play!)
- "Out with his eyes!" (OUCH!)
- "Jellied eel and rotten oranges!" (BLUCK!)
- "Roast rat!"

KING LEAR
Starring Alex

TIME: OLD-TIMEY ENGLAND
SETTING: THE KINGDOM
  (A.K.A. THE REEL LIVING ROOM)
CHARACTERS:
  KING LEAR (THE FATHER)
  THREE DAUGHTERS:
  GONERIL (THE OLDEST...THAT'S ME!)
  REGAN
  CORDELIA (THE YOUNGEST)

*Before the curtain rises: King Lear is
preening himself, waiting to be flattered.
He sits, looking at a map.*

King Lear: *(Why do I have to remind Dad
three times? Stage directions say 'Point
to map'!)* 'Tis time I remove myself from
public life. I wish to give each of thee, my
three daughters, a parcel of my kingdom.
This will depend upon how much each of
you loves me.

Goneril: Shall I compare thee to a summer's
day? *(Good line!)* Thou art more—

Stevie: Alex, quit showing off!

Me: What? That's a real line from Shakespeare. *(I should know!)*

Stevie: Well, it sounds like *Romeo and Juliet,* not *King Lear.*

Joey: Sick! It's from an ooey-gooey love poem!

Dad: Are we going to do this scene or not?

Regan: OK, I love thee more than all four of the seasons, not just one day in summer.

Goneril: I love thee more than meat loves salt.

Regan: Well, I love thee more than meat loves special sauce, lettuce, and a bunch of other stuff on a sesame-seed bun. My love is supersize!

Me: Hey, no fair. Dad, she's making it sound like an old hamburger commercial, not Shakespeare. *(Since when is Stevie the Shakespeare expert?)*

Stevie: Don't look at me. You're the one who loves Dad like meat. I'm just following your lead. You always say to ad-lib.

Goneril: *(Getting down on one knee in front of King Lear.)* I love you more than the ocean has water, more than the sky has stars.

24

Regan: *(Breaking into song.)*

> *My love is warmer than the warmest sunshine,*
> *Softer than a sigh. . . .*

Me: Um, last time I checked, *King Lear* was
not a musical. *(Or a comedy!)*

Joey: Then when do I get a line? You guys
are the greedy sisters, fighting
over all Dad's, I mean, King Lear's, stuff.
Doesn't the good daughter get to say
any words?

Me: Just be happy you didn't have to be an
eggplant.

Dad: OK, Cordelia. Your turn. Read your line.

Cordelia: I can hardly breathe for all this
odious hot air that fills thy room.

Joey: What's *odious* mean?

Stevie and Me: *(Holding noses.)* Stinky!

King Lear: My youngest, you have been
strangely silent. Have you no tender musings
on your love for me?

Cordelia: My love for you, dear Father, is
as a daughter's should be. No more, no less.

25

King Lear: Thou art a boil, a plague-sore, an embossed carbuncle in my corrupted blood. Away with you! Cast thee from my sight forever!

Joey: *(Being dragged from room.)* Hey! What did I do? You mean I get sent away? I thought I was the only one who really loved King Lear.

Stevie: You're still banished!

Joey: No fair. You guys told me I was the good one.

Goneril and Regan: *(Snickering.)* More for us! More for us!

Cordelia: What stugly upsisters you have proven to be. Off with their heads!

Me: You're supposed to say, "A pox on you."

Cordelia: Chicken pox on you!

Me and Stevie: *(In fits of giggles while dragging Joey, a.k.a. Cordelia, from room.)*

Lights go down as Cordelia is banished, stage left. Quick curtain.

Joey: Wait! We're not done. Nobody got stabbed or poisoned or anything.

Me: That's 'cause we lost the plastic dagger.

Joey: Couldn't we just use a spoon or something?

Goneril: How daft! King Lear was lying in his bedchamber, unaware, never guessing he was about to be *spooned* to death!

Regan: Then, when Goneril saw her own image reflected upside down in the spoon, she keeled over and died.

Goneril: Thou thinks thee so clever, but thou art not the least bit funny.

King Lear: *(Collapsing on couch.)* Give an old man some peace!

The Three Sisters

Even though I like *King Lear,* I'm still not thrilled about being related to crazy Hezzy McNutty. Still, I guess I can see why she stopped her wagon when she got here. Take one look at the mountains, and you'd never want to leave, either.

The best view is from a window right in our shower. No lie. When you get up in the morning and look out, the first thing you see are the Cascades, with three snowcapped peaks. They're really volcanoes, called the Three Sisters.

Just like Alex, me, and Joey.

South Sister is the youngest one, like Joey. It's only twenty-five thousand years old. Then there's Middle Sister (me, of course). And North Sister reminds me of Alex. You never know when she's going to erupt (the sister, not the volcano!), especially lately. She's been auditioning for some play at school, and I swear she's gotten bossier by the minute.

So I'm taking a shower, and there are the mountains looking all picture-postcardy, like you could just stick a stamp on that view and send it to somebody you love. In the morning, when the sun hits just right, the snow looks like it just put on some blush, and in the evening, lots of times the mountains look eerie blue, like how I picture Antarctica.

Blue snow.

It sure gets a person dreaming.

Mom wants to get a "real" house someday. I do, too. A house where I wouldn't have to have penguin ballerinas on one-half of the wallpaper (Joey's side) or any wallpaper at all to cover up the hundred-year-old cracks. A house with a room of my own, where I wouldn't have to share a closet or look at names of dead pioneers on the wall or hear Joey say good night to like about a hundred and fifty stuffed animals every night.

And I could keep the light on as long as I want.

But I sure would miss that view.

That's pretty much when Alex starts kicking in the bathroom door, telling me I take the longest showers in the history of History, and that I'd better get out and come to an SCM (Sisters Club Meeting) pronto.

Hey, can I help it if there's a window in the shower?

MYSTERY OF THE MISSING GLITTER NAIL POLISH
Starring Alex

SETTING: ALEX'S BEDROOM
CHARACTERS: THREE SISTERS

Alex, onstage, takes a bow. Lights come up.

Me: *(Picking up shampoo bottle.)* This will be the microphone. Whoever wants to talk has to use the shampoo bottle.

Stevie: Says who?

Me: Says me. Why? Because I'm the oldest. That makes me the director! *(To audience.)* Good evening, ladies and gentlemen. Welcome to Alex's room, where two sisters who do not live in this room (but think they do) are always hanging about.

Joey: You called us in here! For an SCM!

Stevie: Yeah, you got me out of the shower for this? You said it was for the Sisters Club.

Me: Allow me to introduce myself. I am Alex the Actress, star of the Reel Family. That's

Reel, as in film or fishing. Not R-E-A-L, as in *unreal.* I am, for real, the FOBS: First, Oldest, and Best (Reel) Sister! *(Stevie throws a pillow at me; Joey throws a slipper.)* Please refrain from throwing rotten fruit and other objects such as pillows and slippers at the actors.

Stevie: *(Takes shampoo bottle.)* I have a question. How come you always get to go first when we have the Sisters Club?

Me: First is best!

Stevie: You're conceited.

Me: Confident. *(Taking shampoo bottle back.)* Tonight's drama is a mystery. I have called you here to help me solve the Mystery of the Missing Glitter Nail Polish. As the drama unfolds, we will round up the usual suspects and discover WHO is the culprit. Who stole the glitter nail polish from big sister Alex's room?

Joey: *(Pointing to Stevie.)* She did.

Stevie: *(Pointing to Joey.)* She did.

Me: I see we have a stalemate. Let's call in

Sherlock Holmes. *(Putting on houndstooth cap with earflaps, holding out crayon for pipe, and propping Sock Monkey up on chair.)*

Me: *(To Sock Monkey.)* My dear Watson, we must ask the suspects to hold out their hands. *(Joey holds out her hands; Stevie sits on hers.)* What's this I see, old chap?

Sock Monkey: I do believe we have caught BOTH suspects! *(Takes up Joey's hand.)*

Me: Here I see minute traces of a highly reflective decorative material. Suspect Number Two has proven her guilt by concealing her hands altogether. Yes, Watson, I do believe the mystery is solved— in record time, at that.

Sock Monkey: What's the punishment?

Me: The punishment, you say? The two shall hereby be banned from this room forever unless given permission *in writing* to enter.

Joey: How can we have the Sisters Club if we can't even come in your room?

Stevie: It was for science! I was helping Joey with constellations.

Me: And is it not written in the stars that you shall never enter this room when I am not here? I'm serious, you guys—stay out! *(Stevie rolls her eyes. Joey jumps up and grabs the shampoo bottle.)*

Joey: How come you're like this now? You hardly ever play with us anymore. We never get to have fun.

Me: Hello! I'm twelve and three-quarters. I'm almost a teenager, not a baby.

Joey: Well, how come you won't let us touch your stuff now? Not just nail polish. Even your old Barbies you don't play with anymore.

Me: Reality check! They're M-I-N-E. Just like this nail polish. *(Holding up Joey's hand.)* The evidence, Watson. The evidence. I rest my case.

Fondue Sue

One Thursday, Mom put on The Hat at dinner.

"Da-da-da-da!" my dad crowed, like he was a human trumpet.

I guess I better tell you about The Hat. We're talking really embarrassing. See, there's this jester hat my dad wore when he played King Lear for real. It looks kind of like a droopy crown with bells on the ends. When somebody has something important to say in our family, they have to put on The Hat and announce it like they're the town crier or something.

Me, I'm more of a sticky-note-on-the-fridge kind of person.

"I have some news," Mom began.

"Good news or bad news?" asked Alex. Joey sat up straighter.

"Good news! I'm going back to work. A real acting job. No more bit parts at the Raven. This is my big break. Are you ready for this?"

Mom whipped out a dopey-looking striped apron that said FONDUE SUE in big fat letters with rolling pins flying around in the background.

"Your name's not Sue," said Joey.

"I'm going to be on *TV*!" said Mom. "I just got my own cooking show. This is my character, Fondue Sue."

"How is this possible?" asked Alex. "You can't even cook!"

"What do you mean? I cook for this family almost every night, in case you haven't noticed," said Mom.

"Yeah, potatoes from a box and spaghetti from a can," Alex said. "They'll have to call your show *The Art of Opening a Can*!"

Root beer went up my nose. I had to duck to avoid Joey's mashed-potato-from-a-box spray across the table.

"Girls, c'mon now," Dad said. "Let's try to be supportive. This is a big opportunity for Mom."

"Mom, you know what fondue is, right?" Know-It-All Alex asked Mom. "Cheese glop! Fondue is French for cheese glop."

"Mom. Name the five food groups," said Little Miss Homework (Joey).

"Meats, Vegetables, Fruits. Let's see . . . pretzels and things like that go at the top, right? Junk food?"

"Mo-om. Pretzels are not a food group! They call it Oils, not Junk Food. They teach us that in third grade. At the *beginning* of the year."

"Look, they're going to give me all the ingredients," said Mom. "I won't even have to chop a single toe of garlic or sift my own flour. All I have to do is smile and point and read the prompts. Maybe a little stirring and mixing. How hard could it be?"

"Mom. News flash. Garlic doesn't have toes," I said.

"Witches stir and mix things," said Joey. "Why don't you just be a witch?"

"Hey, I know! You could be a TV anchorwoman!" said Alex. "Or a meteorologist on the eleven o'clock news. They smile and point. And you get to wear a matching two-piece suit, not a dopey apron with a funny fondue name."

"But I'll be acting," Mom said. "I don't have to know how to cook. That's why it's called *acting*."

Mom took off the *King Lear* hat and set it on the table, all crumply-like.

"This is my chance to make some real money. We could save for a house. A real house of our own. Not this crickety old monster with the falling-down roof."

"We don't have crickets," Joey said. "Or monsters."

"And we're used to the saggy old roof. It's like it's leaning down to hug us," Alex said. "And these crooked old floors remember our footsteps."

I didn't want Mom to be a goofy chef on TV any more than Joey or Alex, but I could tell it meant a lot to her. So what did I do? I remembered my role as the middle sister, the glue, and I rushed in to save the day. "It'll be great, Mom. Don't worry. I can cook dinner. Alex and Joey will help me. Right, you guys?" Nobody answered.

"Just think," said Alex. "You'll be like that weird lady on the old Mary Tyler Moore reruns. The one with the corny cooking show."

"Cooking shows don't have to be corny anymore," Mom said, defending herself. "They're hip now."

"Mom!" I told her. "It's not even hip to *say* 'hip'!"

"Dad, you remember," Alex continued. "The goofy lady who was always making flambé and flan and Florentine stuff. What was her name? Sue Ann?"

"Sue Ann Fondue?" Joey and I sprayed each other with laughter—and more mashed potatoes.

"Say it, don't spray it," said Alex, making us crack up and spray all the more.

"Sheesh," said Mom. "This cooking thing is going to be a lot more complicated than I thought."

The No-Joy of Cooking

I should have known the Reel Family was in big trouble as soon as I laid eyes on the *Joy of Cooking.*

It was the very next day after Martha-Stewart-formerly-known-as-Mom made her big announcement. She hauled this giant book out of the back of a cupboard we use like once a year, since you can only reach it by standing on a chair. The book was covered in dust that dated back to the *Titanic.*

Mom dusted it off. She cracked open the spine.

"When did you get that?" I asked her, in between choking on one-hundred-year-old dust particles.

"It was a gift. When your dad and I got married."

"Is it an antique?" asked Joey.

"It looks brand-new," I said. (Minus the *Titanic* dust, that is.)

"I wonder why," said Alex.

"Ha, ha," said Mom, not laughing.

"I thought you were *acting*," said Alex. "I thought you didn't have to know how to cook."

"Well, I should know something about it," said Mom. "I have to get into my role, after all."

There was no stopping her.

For seven days straight, we ate Mom's cooking. She dished it up; we choked it down. Each night was more disgusting than the one before.

"What is this stuff, anyway?" I couldn't help asking that first night.

"Beef tournedos," said Mom.

"I know why they call it 'tornado,'" Joey said. She pointed to the kitchen mess, cracking up. It did look like a disaster area.

All week, there were Quick Potato Dumplings that needed dumping and Cheese Puffs that didn't puff. There was Chicken à la King without any king and

41

Eggs Benedict that Benedict Arnold himself would not have eaten.

By the fifth night of cooking, Mom stared at the cheese-puff-stained cover of the cookbook. "I don't know why they call this the *'Joy' of Cooking*," said Mom. Joey and I rolled our eyes at each other. Mom looked at the author's name on the cookbook. "Who is this Irma S. Rombauer person, anyway? She is going to hear from me."

This is Mom's favorite saying. Whenever she doesn't like something, somebody is going to hear from her.

"I think Irma S. Rombauer is dead, Mom," I said. "On account of the book being like a hundred years old." I opened the book to a random page, looking to prove my point. "'Potted Goose,'" I read aloud. "Did they have potted goose in colonial times, when this book was written?" I flipped some more pages. "'Marinated Wild Birds.'"

"Marinated Wild Birds!" Alex shouted. "What kind of person would marinate wild birds? We should throw the book away this second. Before the Sierra Club arrests us."

By the end of the week, we were getting pretty desperate—and pretty hungry.

"I know," Joey said, trying to be helpful. "Why don't you make something we've actually heard of? Like Jell-O. You make really good Jell-O."

Joey could *live* on Jell-O. I'm surprised she doesn't turn into the stuff.

"Ya know, one day we're gonna wake up and there's gonna be a jiggly mass of green stuff in your bed instead of you," I warned. "Invasion of the Jell-O monsters."

Joey grinned—like she thought turning into Jell-O was a good idea.

"How about Tuna Noodle Casserole?" I suggested. "It's easy. Everybody knows how to make Tuna Noodle Casserole. You can't go wrong. Look. It says right here in the *No-Joy of Cooking,* page 529. 'Excellent Emergency Dish.'"

"This *is* an emergency," said Mom.

"And if anything goes wrong, I can always put out the fire," Dad called from the hallway. "I played a fire-fighter back in summer stock one year, remember?"

"Very funny," Mom said. "I'm going to do this, and

it's not going to burn. Do you think maybe something's wrong with our oven?"

"As in *Never Been Used*?" I asked.

"Oh, I see. A whole family of comedians," said Mom. "Too bad they didn't ask me to do stand-up."

That night, Mom minced and whipped and greased and poured and sprinkled and sifted until she had herself one Foolproof Emergency Tuna Noodle Casserole.

"This is good noodle casserole," Alex said, trying to sound encouraging. "Do you think they make noodle casserole on hip TV shows?"

"Not without tuna. I didn't get any tuna in mine," said Joey. I kicked her under the table. "Hey, Stevie kicked me."

"Girls," said Dad.

"I forgot the tuna?" wailed Mom. "I forgot the tuna, didn't I? You can't have Tuna Noodle Casserole without the tuna!"

"It's fine," said Dad. "Yum." For an actor, he wasn't very convincing.

Mom ran to call one of her sisters long-distance.

Like she always does when things are looking worse than hopeless.

"I think I lost five pounds this week," Alex whispered to me.

"I miss potatoes from a box," I said.

"I miss Mom," said Joey.

J-E-L-L-O!
by Joey Reel

Jell-O is my favorite dessert. It comes in rainbow colors. I like the way it wiggles and jiggles and looks like brains. Writing this report made me wonder, What is Jell-O, really? I mean, what's it made of?

So I looked it up.

GROSS!

Jell-O is really gelatin, which is made from animal parts like skin and bones and inside stuff. Bluck!

It's used in foods . . . and film! Double bluck!

I eat film! (But it tastes good.)

(Note to self: Don't tell the Queen of Animal Rights, sister Alex.) Or do! ~S

In closing, I would like to say that Jell-O is one of the only things my mom makes that I actually like. When I'm sick, she always makes lime Jell-O, and it helps me feel better. I hope I never get sick anymore, because who is going to make me lime Jell-O?

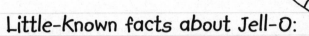

Little-known facts about Jell-O:

1. Jell-O is over a hundred years old (older than Mom's <u>Joy of Cooking</u>!).
2. The 413,997,403 packages of Jell-O made in one year would stretch three-fifths of the way around the globe.
3. Immigrants at Ellis Island were served Jell-O to say, "Welcome to America."
4. A bowl of wiggly Jell-O has brain waves that are the same as grown-ups'.
5. Astronaut Shannon Lucid kept track of time on the Mir Space Station by wearing pink socks and eating Jell-O every Sunday.

Things to put in Jell-O:
- Sprinkles
- Mini-marshmallows
- Yogurt
- Anything that floats
- A note to your sister!

Things NOT to put in Jell-O:

- Grapes (They sink.)
- Grapefruit (It stinks.)
- Gummy worms (You can't see them.)
- Barbie shoes (My mom really did that once!)

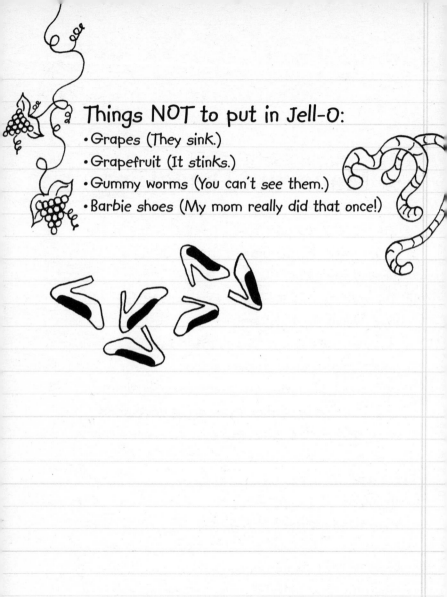

Macaroni Disaster

I could not face eating cold pizza or leftover Chinese takeout for dinner one more time. Ever since Mom had gone back to work, we had not eaten together as a family—not once. Alex had caught Play Fever and was practicing for her *Beauty and the Beast* audition nonstop. She'd even stopped coming to Sisters Club Meetings! And Dad was busy building props for *Beauty* and directing a play next door at the Raven almost every evening.

The closest we could get to being a family was Joey and me eating soggy cornflakes for dinner while we watched Mom on TV. The first time Joey saw Fondue Sue, her eyes almost popped out—like some alien in a striped apron had taken over our mom. She had (matching) little dishes full of chopped-diced-minced things and powdery things, like magic potions that she tossed and flung, stirred, sautéed, and coddled.

"But Mom can't even crack an egg," said Joey.

"She can on TV," I said.

Joey looked down at her dismal cornflakes, which now looked more like papier-mâché. "Those stuffed, wrapped thingies actually look good!" Joey said, leaning into the television.

I decided it was time for me to step in and make an RFD—Real Family Dinner? *Reel* Family Dinner! I mean, how hard could it be to cook? But I wasn't about to do it all by myself.

First I tried to convince Alex. I even told her it was an Emergency SCM. In the past, that meant to drop everything and meet in Alex's room in two seconds.

She didn't even look up—she just mumbled she'd be downstairs in a few minutes (more like one hour!). *After* practicing her lines for her *Beauty and the Beast* audition, which she did like a million and one times a day.

Then I went to find Joey on Planet Jell-O (under the piano). She'd been living there all week, eating (what else?) lime Jell-O. It's all I've seen her eat since Mom became Fondue Sue (besides the before-mentioned papier-mâché cornflakes).

"Do you think the pioneers ate Jell-O?" she asked me.

"No. The pioneers were smart. They knew that if you ate too much lime Jell-O, your face and hands would turn green, and your ears would jiggle and fall off."

"Would not!"

"Would, too! What are you doing under there, anyway?

"I had to get inside my covered wagon because it was raining so hard."

"Well, it stopped raining now. Come help me chop wood to start a cooking fire."

"But the wood's all wet. It won't light."

"C'mon, Joey! It's Family Dinner! Mom would not want us moping around feeling all sorry for ourselves."

Joey stuck her lip out.

"Stick that lip out any farther, and a chicken'll come lay an egg on it."

She pulled the lip in. I guess she did not want chickens roosting on her face.

"Don't be stubborn. If I told you it's for homework, would you help?"

"Maybe."

"It's for homework."

"What kind of homework?"

"Science homework. Pretend we have to save something endangered."

"Like what?"

"Like we're saving the Family Dinner from going extinct around here."

"Can we make Mac and Cheese?"

"Sure, Duck. We can make whatever you want. Sweet Potato Soufflé, Crêpes Suzette, Jellied Eel, Roast Rat—anything. Just *not* Beef Tornado."

"And it can't come from a box."

Joey and I headed toward the kitchen, a Sisters Club of two. Joey sat at the table and wrote some more in her notebook. She wasn't exactly helping, but at least I stopped her from living under the piano.

I opened the refrigerator. Three hairy peaches, green cheese, and an art project. "Hey! What are your constellations doing in the fridge?" I asked Joey.

"The glitter nail polish has to get hard."

"Duck! Go put this on the table."

Pout-face Joey put down her notebook and took her constellations to the (not-being-used) dining room table. I opened the butter door. "No butter. Just film."

"Did you know Jell-O is really gooey stuff made from animal parts and they use it in film?" said Joey.

"Gross! Well, we're not eating film, even if it is made of Jell-O! OK, forget the butter. We'll use eggs, milk, and cheese. That's a food group, right?"

"Green cheese? P.U. We're going to eat green cheese?"

"We'll cut off the mold. Just like the pioneers!" Joey's face lit up when I said the magic word.

She scribbled some more in her notebook.

I poured the noodles into the skillet and grated the cheese and beat the eggs and stirred the milk. All Joey did was play with the saltshaker.

"Joey! You're not helping. Here. Put two drops of hot sauce in."

"Whatever you say, Betty Cracker."

"I said two drops! Not a flood! That stuff is really hot. Give it."

I stirred everything together. "Look. You turned the Mac and Cheese all orange."

"It doesn't look right anyway," Joey told me.

She was right. The macaroni looked too small. And burned. Not plump and fluffy like Dad's used to be in the good old days (B.B., Before *Beauty*). I'd seen Dad melt the cheese over macaroni in the skillet a hundred times. What had I done wrong?

"Where's Alex?"

"Not here."

"Is she still practicing for tryouts? All she cares about is that play!"

"I know," said Joey. "Hey, let's make the whole dinner orange! We can have orange Popsicles and orange juice and stuff. Then they'll think we did it on purpose. Like a theme!"

I wanted to like her idea. I wanted her to feel like she was a big help. "OK, how about Mac and Cheese and orange carrots and orange juice."

"And don't forget dessert," said Joey. "Orange Jell-O! *Orange* you glad I didn't say banana?"

"Oh, brother."

"Don't you mean sister?" she asked.

I spread a tablecloth over the coffee table. "Let's sit on the floor, Japanese style."

Joey was in charge of the (all-orange) centerpiece. A half-melted pumpkin candle, a snow globe of the Golden Gate Bridge (minus the snow), a horn-toed lizard she got at the zoo, and socks.

"I hope they like orange in Japan," Joey said.

Then everything started to happen all at once. Mom yelled, "I'm home!" Dad yelled, "What's that smell?" Alex made an appearance (better late than never), peeking under pot lids and snitching carrots from the bowl. Some help.

Joey was running around, collecting all the dirty dishes and pots and pans and putting them in the sink to soak. She squeezed like five million gallons of dishwashing liquid in there. I know she was trying to help, but it looked more like she was building the Eiffel Tower in the kitchen sink.

I checked the table. Everything looked OK—pretty good even, minus the Mac and Cheese, which looked super-strange, like astronaut food or something.

"Who made this?" asked Mom (minus any yummy noises).

"Crêpes Stevette," said Joey, not taking any credit for the orange mess.

"Um . . . why are there socks on the table?" Alex asked.

"Because they're orange," said Joey. "It's a theme!"

Everybody stared at their plates. I caught Joey doing the old napkin-under-the-table trick, feeding everything but the Jell-O to her napkin. Did she think I didn't know? I invented that trick.

"C'mon, you guys. It's not like it's *King Lear* jellied eel and rotten oranges." I tried to sound cheerful. But my own plate stared up at me, all orange and lumpy.

"BLUCK! What is *this*?" I asked, pulling a particularly disgusting lump from my Mac and Cheese. "Ooh! It's an *ear*!" Gloppy cheese dropped from its lobe. "Jo-ey!" I couldn't believe I'd been the victim of the Rubber Ear Trick—me, who invented that one, too!

Alex burst out laughing. "There's an ear in your macaroni? Yee-uck. I hope there aren't any elbows in mine." She poked it with a fork. "Or eyeballs."

Joey cracked up.

"Very funny, Duck," I said. "See how hard I'm laughing? Ha, ha, ha, ha, ha," I said, holding the cheesy ear out to her.

"I can't hear you," Joey said.

"Pass the salt," said Alex. "At least it's not orange."

"And it doesn't have ears!" said Joey, cracking herself up all over again.

Dad was first to take a bite. *Crunch!*

Mom tried a mouthful. *Crr-unch!*

Alex swallowed. "Wa-ter," she gasped, holding her throat.

"What's wrong with everybody? This is supposed to be a Family Dinner," I told them. "You know, where we all get to be together, have conversation? Not just eat cereal from a box and watch Mom on TV."

"I think I broke a tooth!" shouted Alex.

Dad wiped his mouth about a hundred and one times with his napkin. Even Dad was using the old napkin trick!

"I'm not one to talk when it comes to cooking—" Mom started.

"I made it just like Dad does!" I protested.

"Stevie, honey, you did *boil* the macaroni first,

57

didn't you?" Dad asked. "*Before* you put it in the skillet?"

Joey looked at me and burst out laughing. I mean really lost it this time.

"Carrots, anyone?" I asked, not even cracking a smile.

Suds-O-Rama

Just when I thought Family Dinner couldn't get any worse, Alex said, "Hey, what's that sound?"

"It's the fridge gurgling," said Mom.

"Sometimes it does 'The Star-Spangled Banner,'" said Dad.

Everybody was laughing except me. I wasn't laughing, because I saw something. Something moving. Creeping out of the kitchen. Right toward me. Inching closer and closer.

Not a disgusting rat or giant termite or million-legged centipede or anything like that. It was a mountain of white, foamy, bubbly, frothy *soapsuds,* floating down the hall like a giant bubble bath coming at us.

"I'll be right back," I said, and raced for the kitchen. Then I screamed.

Alex and Joey came running, with Mom and Dad right behind.

Suds were pouring out of the sink, slithering across the counter, sliding down the cabinets and across the floor, and swimming down the hall like some cumulus cloud of foamy froth.

"Awesome!" Alex said, like she was admiring a work of art. "Which one of you hairy stinkpodes left the water on?"

"Don't just stand there!" I told her, pawing my way through piles of suds, miles of suds. "TURN! OFF! THE! WATER!"

"This is cool. Like a car wash, without the car!" Alex said.

Joey yelled, "Giant bubbles! Whee!" She picked up a handful of suds and blew on it. Bubbles flew through the air and landed on Alex's head.

"Not the hair!" Alex said. "OK, you're in for it now, Little Sister!"

"Look out! Attack of Mr. Bubble!" I screamed in a food-fight voice, and pushed some suds toward Alex.

"Take that!" Alex flicked some back at me.

"Hey! You flicked me!" I yelled. "That does it." I grabbed a clump of suds in each hand and flung them snowball-style at Alex.

She grabbed two handfuls of suds and flung them back at me, underhand. Before I knew it, I was smack-dab in the middle of a giant bubble bath with my sisters!

"Ooh, I feel some sliding down my back," said Alex.

"So? I got some up my nose. See?" said Joey.

Mom jumped in, pretending she was on one of her TV shows. "This is Fondue Sue, reporting to you live from the home of the Reel Sisters, where they've just made the world's largest cappuccino, as you can see from the cloud of foam I'm standing in. . . ."

Dad couldn't stand to just watch. He made himself a bubble beard à la Abe Lincoln and started reciting the Gettysburg Address. "Fourscore and seven years ago . . ."

While Dad was imitating our forefather, Mom was making a soapsuds statue.

"Is it a snowman?" Alex asked.

"Is it a poodle?" I asked.

"It's Mickey Mouse," said Joey.

Mom started to laugh. And laugh. Then we all couldn't help laughing, too.

"Mom, what is it?" I asked, flinging a handful of suds back into the sink.

"I just couldn't help thinking," Mom said in between laugh gasps, "our kitchen hasn't been this clean since Hepzibiah McNutty herself lived here!"

Family Dinner Report
by Joey Reel

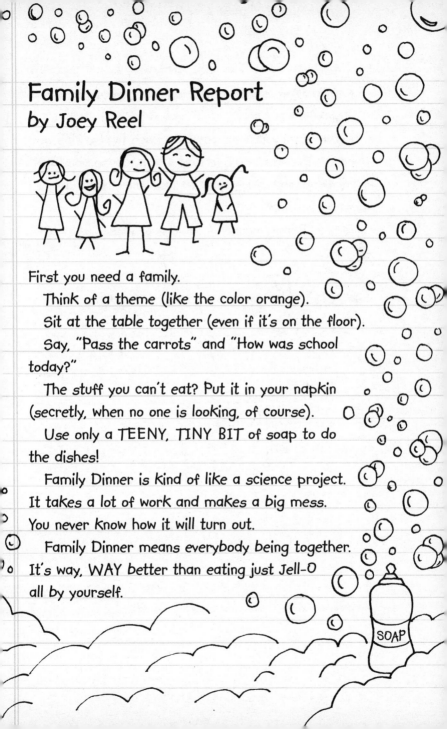

First you need a family.

Think of a theme (like the color orange).

Sit at the table together (even if it's on the floor).

Say, "Pass the carrots" and "How was school today?"

The stuff you can't eat? Put it in your napkin (secretly, when no one is looking, of course).

Use only a TEENY, TINY BIT of soap to do the dishes!

Family Dinner is kind of like a science project. It takes a lot of work and makes a big mess. You never know how it will turn out.

Family Dinner means everybody being together. It's way, WAY better than eating just Jell-O all by yourself.

SOAP

Family Dinner makes you not want to live under the piano.

After Family Dinner, your stomach hurts. Not because the food was so bad, not because you ate a lot of orange stuff, but because you ended up laughing so hard.

A+ for Family Dinner!

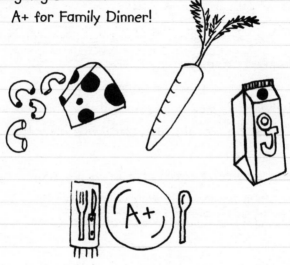

Dear Sock Monkey:
I have to go to school today, and I keep staring at my closet, but there's nothing to wear. What should I do?
~Bathrobe Beauty (a.k.a. Stevie)

Dear B.B.:
I'm partial to brown, with an accent of red, but choose a color that makes you happy, and you'll feel good about yourself. Whatever you do, don't borrow anything that belongs to Alex!
✳ Sock Monkey ✳

65

The Power of the Sweater

I was more than ready to get back to school on Monday. After the Macaroni Disaster, even cafeteria food was starting to look good to me.

Only one problem. I had nothing to wear.

"Nothing to wear," I said out loud to my closet.

I was standing flamingo-style (on one foot) in my blue jeans and favorite flannel pajama top (covered with cupcakes), staring at a bunch of hangers.

Joey wrinkled her nose at me. "You're starting to sound like A-L-E-X."

"And you're starting to sound like M-O-M."

I stared at the hangers some more. "You just don't understand, Little Sister." Joey wrinkled her nose again.

"Stop wrinkling," I told her. "You look like a rhinoceros."

I went down the hall to Alex's room. I could hear her downstairs banging away on the piano. Only Alex would play Mozart at seven o'clock in the morning.

"You better not go in there without asking!" Joey warned. "Alex said!"

I went in anyway.

Joey stood with her toes just outside the doorway, so technically she did not step into Alex's room. "It's your life!" she told me.

I had another idea, a much better idea, and one that did not involve trespassing. I headed straight for the laundry room, where I could hear the *whump, whump* of the dryer.

I quietly click-opened the dryer and took out Alex's soft, fuzzy red chenille sweater with the big pink star—her favorite. I used to have the same sweater in green, but I washed it with the red one and it came out looking like spaghetti in a blender.

A part of me *knew* Alex was drying the sweater so she could wear it today. But I told myself she had a million other sweaters. I told myself I was sick of being invisible. I told myself the lump of guilt in the pit of my stomach was just the protein bar I'd eaten for breakfast.

I yanked the sweater from the dryer. Perfect! All cozy-warm and soft as kitten fur, with an apple-clean smell. I shrugged it on. The pink star grinned up at me.

For once, I would be the star, not Alex. I hurried and covered it up with my coat before anybody could see. I grabbed my backpack and ran down the street to my friend Olivia's house, hoping to catch a ride.

I tried not to think about Alex or what would happen after school when I got home. Nothing mattered except for that moment. What a great morning. And it was going to be a great day.

I, middle sister Stevie, had the power of the sweater.

This Is Just to Say

During Language Arts, Ms. Carter-Dunne gave us ten minutes to pick a famous poem in our book. "I want everyone to choose a poem you like, then use it as a model to write one of your own. Look at the poem's style. Think about how it's written. Let the poem inspire you."

I flipped back and forth through the pages as fast as I could.

"This is an in-class assignment, people. I'll give you time to write, then we'll read some of them out loud."

Out loud! A.k.a. *in front of the whole class*! I broke out in a sweat just thinking about it.

I flipped some more. First I saw a Russian poem, but it had the word *breast*. No way was I going to say "breast" in front of a bunch of fifth-grade boys (half the class!). I almost picked a haiku about trees, but nobody gets a good grade for a haiku. It's only three lines.

Olivia picked "We Real Cool" right off the bat.

"No fair!" I told her. "What if I want that one?"

"Pick this one." She opened to a page and pointed.

"No way. The guy says he feels like an eggplant." That's when I saw the plums. Plums beat eggplants any day! (Just ask Joey.) So I picked a poem by a plum eater, a Mr. William Carlos Williams.

This Is Just to Say

I have eaten
the plums
that were in
the icebox

and which
you were probably
saving
for breakfast

Forgive me
they were delicious
so sweet
and so cold

I don't know what it is with me and poetry—why it was freaking me out. It looks simple enough, but I had to read it over and over about a bazillion times. Then it hit me. Like Mr. William Famous Williams *himself* was talking to me, Stevie Reel. It's weird, I know, because he was talking about plums, but somehow he knew just how I felt—about the sweater.

I'm Sorry

I have taken
your sweater
that was in
the dryer

and which
you were probably
going to wear
today

Forgive me
I spilled chocolate on it
It wasn't fair
I used to have the same one

But I still enjoyed
how everyone said
I looked better in it than you

After we had quiet time to write our poems (with Ms. Carter-Dunne looking over our shoulders half the time), she asked me to read my poem aloud in front of the whole class.

My poem.

Why did she have to pick me? I tried to tell her it was private. I tried to tell her it really wasn't meant to be read aloud (to a bunch of immature fifth-graders!).

I tried to tell her, but she said, "Nonsense, Stevie. Your poem is a perfect example for the rest of the class. It's just what I'm looking for. It's inspiring. No need to be shy."

Easy for her to say. Why do teachers think that telling you not to be shy will make you not feel shy? Guess what, Ms. Carter-Dunne, Queen of Reading-Aloud-in-Front-of-the-Whole-World? It just makes it worse!

So I, Stevie Reel, who hates acting (despite being a direct descendant of Hepzibiah McNutty), who hates standing up in front of people, had to stand in front of the whole class with sweat circles under my arms (in Alex's sweater!) and read my poem to twenty-nine

pairs of squinty eyes (that's fifty-eight eyes, guys)
while trying not to spit or spray or choke on the last
line. Or turn ten shades of red. Or pass out from
embarrassment.

At least I didn't have to say "breast"!

Why not a haiku?
Haiku's not embarrassing. . . .
O, for the haiku!

Copycat
by Joey Reel

I wanted to do some fifth-grade homework, like Stevie. So I snooped in her school folder. I found a poem she wrote. (She copied some famous guy!)

In third grade, Mr. B. won't let us copy. When I asked Stevie, she said:

1. I better stop snooping in her stuff
   — but it's not like it's her diary.

Hello! It's still private! ~S

2. She didn't copy anybody.

3. I better not show Alex.
   I'm going to, of course!

I just got INSPIRED. ~S

By plums? —J

If you show her, I swear I'll put salt on your cereal, hide your 150 stuffed animals, and glue your hair to your pillow! ~S

My poem is about sisters. (NOT sweaters!)
   Only I didn't copy any famous guy.
   And I didn't get inspired by plums.

Oh, brother. ~S

Hey, stop stealing my pen! —J

Sisters Are Forever
(a poem by Joey Reel)

Sisters copy.
Sisters talk to sock monkeys!
Sisters steal stuff and don't ask.
Sisters fight.
Sisters call you Jell-O names.
What goes away but always comes back?
Sisters!

Dear Sock Monkey:
I have a big audition for <u>Beauty</u> <u>and</u>
<u>the</u> <u>Beast</u> tomorrow. I'm so nervous
I can't sleep. Help!
    Sleepless in South Oregon (a.k.a. Alex)

Dear Sleepless:
Close your eyes, take a
deep breath, and try
counting sock monkeys!
Soon you'll be relaxed,
and... zzzzzzzzzz.
    * Sock Monkey *

76

ZITS
Starring Alex

Me: I had my audition today, Sock Monkey.
For the best part ever. Beauty, in *Beauty
and the Beast.*

Sock Monkey: Well, I didn't think you were
the Beast!

Me: Thank you! That's why I love you so much.
Mww! Mww! (Kissing sounds.)

Sock Monkey: Then what's wrong?

Me: I so did *not* get the part.

Sock Monkey: What do you mean?

Me: First of all, I didn't have my lucky
sweater.

Sock Monkey: How come?

Me: Because my evil, wicked un-stepsister
Stevie stole it from the dryer.

Sock Monkey: That's evil! Wicked! Very
stepsister-y of her.

Me: I know. But that's not even the worst part.

Sock Monkey: Oh, no. What's the worst part?

Me: I messed up my lines.

Sock Monkey: Everybody makes mistakes.

Me: Not like this!

Sock Monkey: It can't be all that bad.

Me: It is. Or as Beauty would say, "'Tis a sorrow. 'Tis a tragedy."

Sock Monkey: What happened?

Me: OK, see, there's this guy I like. . . . His name is Scott Howell. He's in Drama Club, and he's really good at acting, and I know he's going to get the part of Beast.

Sock Monkey: So you want to star in the play with him, right?

Me: More than anything. Maybe he would like me if we got to practice together and everything.

Sock Monkey: You can do it!

Me: But wait. I haven't told you the bad part.

Sock Monkey: Go on.

Me: We were practicing reading our parts, and I kept noticing this zit he had on his face.

Sock Monkey: Gross!

Me: I tried not to look at it. . . .

Sock Monkey: Maybe he didn't see you see it.

Me: I wish! That's not it. We were saying our
lines back and forth for the audition, and
I was going along fine. It's the part where
Beauty is trapped at her father's house,
and she has a dream that Beast is dying.
She wakes up and has a revelation.

The line goes, "I am indeed quite wicked
to cause so much grief to Beast, who
has shown me nothing but kindness. Is it
his fault that he is so ugly and has so
few wits?"

Sock Monkey: What's wrong with that?

Me: I messed up! Now I'll never get the part,
and Scott Howell will hate me forever.
Here's what I said. No lie. I said, "Is it his
fault that he is so ugly and has so few
zits?"

Ha, ha, ha, ha, ha! *(Laughter from evil un-*
stepsisters offstage.)

Talking to Doors

Alex flung open the door. She glared at us with mice eyes, all puffy like she had been crying. She started swearing at us in Shakespeare. "You gore-bellied, hasty-witted harpies!" she yelled.

"Don't you mean hasty-*zitted* harpies?" I said, cracking up even more.

"How long have you been out there? You guys heard every word I said, didn't you?"

"Scott Towel has zits!" said Joey. She lost it, giggling like it was the funniest thing ever.

Joey's giggling egged me on. "Oh, Sock Monkey. I adore you. I love you," I said, imitating Alex. "You're just an old sock, but you look just like my boyfriend, Scott Towel! Kiss, kiss, kiss."

"*Howell!* It's Scott *Howell*! If you're going to eaves-drop, get it right." Alex narrowed her mean eyes at us. "I wish I never had a sister. That goes for BOTH of you."

For once, we knew to keep quiet.

"And don't think I forgot you stole my sweater, Stevie. My lucky sweater! Where is it? I mean it. You better give it back this minute. And Joey, don't think I forgot you. You're a dankish elf-skinned clodpole! No better than Stevie. If Mom was here, I'd—"

"I am not an elf or whatever!" said Joey.

"I hope you both turn to stone. Just like Beauty's evil sisters in the fairy tale. I'd like you much better as statues—that's for sure!"

Joey looked at me like she didn't know whether to laugh or cry.

"Out, vile jelly!" Alex shouted. "A pox of wrinkles on thee!"

She slammed the door in our faces without waiting to get her sweater back. *Thonk!* The door slamming knocked a picture off the wall in the hallway. A picture of Alex when she was a mushroom in *Mushroom in the Rain,* her kindergarten play. I wonder if she heard the thud from inside her room.

"You're still a mushroom!" I shouted, only because it sounded good. Silence. Was she still listening?

"Nothing short of a miracle will turn a wicked and envious heart!" she shouted through the door, quoting her beloved Beauty.

"You're the big meanie," Joey said. "Puke-face dung heap," she yelled, trying to swear in Shakespeare.

"Rrrrr! Sisters make me crazy," yelled Alex.

"Ditto!" I yelled back.

"Double ditto!" yelled Joey, even though she doesn't know what it means.

We both sat on Joey's bed (after moving about a hundred stuffed animals), staring at the mess that used to be Alex's sweater.

"Stevie?" Joey asked.

"Not now, Duck. I have to think."

"About what?"

"What to do about Alex, the sweater—everything."

"She was calling us evil Jell-O and stuff!"

"That was just Shakespeare. She always spits out Shakespeare when she's mad."

"She doesn't even know you wrecked the sweater yet. She just thinks you stole it."

"Don't tell, Duck! She's going to kill me when she finds out," I said. "Or at the very least, turn me into a zitty-faced stinkard!"

"She'll see." Joey pointed to the mess of yarn on my bed that used to be Alex's sweater. "It looks like a bird's nest. What happened?"

"I told you. The tag was itching me. So I cut it off. I do it all the time on my own stuff. All I did was pull this one thread, and next thing I knew the whole thing came undone," I said.

"Maybe we could sew it," Joey suggested. "Mom could help us."

"How? She's not even here."

"Maybe we could make it into something else."

"What? Like a Sweater Monkey?"

"Like a scarf, or a pillow for her room."

"Hey, that's a great idea, Duck. I think I can make a pillow with the star on the front. At least she'd have *something*."

All afternoon, I tried to make a sweater pillow for Alex. It looked more like a bed for Sock Monkey. It didn't help that Joey kept bugging me. "Duck," I asked her, "don't you have some pretend homework to do?"

Finally, when I finished my not-a-pillow creation, I held it up for Joey to see. "I don't know, Joey," I said. "Maybe I should just never tell Alex—"

"Never tell Alex what?" said Sock Monkey (a.k.a. Alex) from the doorway. I hid the sweater thingy under my pillow.

"Nothing," I said as Alex came into the room.

"I'm not blind, you know. Something happened to my sweater. You lost it, didn't you? Or you left it at school and somebody stole it? Which is it?"

"I made you something," I said, sounding lame. I took it out from under my pillow.

"A pot holder?" said Alex. "You made me a *pot holder*?" She said "pot holder" like it was a bad word or something.

"I was trying to make a pillow, but . . ."

"This is all that's left of the sweater? My lucky sweater? I had to audition for *Beauty* without it, and now I probably didn't get the part, all because of you." Alex ran down the hall to her room, clutching Sock Monkey. She slammed the door again.

"Do you think I should go talk to her?" I asked Joey.

"Nope," Joey said.

I tiptoed down the hall anyway. I knocked on Alex's door. Lately I've been talking more to doors than to my sister.

"I know you're upset," I said to the door. No answer.

"Alex, c'mon, don't be mad. I'm sorry. I didn't mean to ruin your sweater. All I did was cut out the tag. Honest. And it all came apart. What can I do?"

The door cracked open in the middle of my speech. Sock Monkey poked his button eyes through the crack and said, "You owe Alex one sweater. You better go buy her a new one. And she is not kidding. She means it." All I could see of Alex were her teeth smiling sweetly through the door crack, like she was acting for a toothpaste commercial or something.

"You've got to be joking," I told her. "I don't have any money. That sweater cost like thirty dollars. Where am I going to get thirty dollars?"

"You figure it out," Sock Monkey squeaked. The door closed, not with a slam this time but more like a quiet click. It felt creepy—worse than a slam. Two seconds later the door opened, and she hung a thingy on the doorknob that said SISTER-FREE ZONE.

The door clicked shut again.

"Wait!" I said to the door. Only a slab of dark wood separated us, but it felt like the Great Wall of China. I put my ear to the door, trying to listen to see if she was still standing there, if I heard breathing.

All I heard was the door.

"You do NOT look better than me in that sweater!" said Alex the Door.

How to Swear in Shakespeare

From the often-used vocabulary of Alex Reel, whenever she is around her sisters

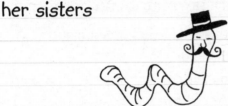

- You quintessence of dust!
- Mad mustachio'd purple-hued maltworm!
- Puke-stocking!
- Valiant flea!
- Dunghill groom!
- Bedlam brainsick duchess!
- Bolting-hutch of beastliness!
- Foul fiend Flibbertigibbet!
- King of codpieces!
- Gross watery pumpion!
- Spotted snake with double tongue!
- A pox of wrinkles (on thee)!
- A bugbear take you!
- A plague o' pickle-herring (upon thee)!

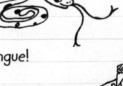

PICKLED HERRING

MEET SCOTT TOWEL
Starring Alex

TIME: AFTER SCHOOL
SETTING: STANDING IN FRONT OF THE DRAMA CLUB
   BULLETIN BOARD
CHARACTERS: ME (ALEX) AND HIM(!)

Him: So, think you'll get the part of Beauty?

Me: *(It's him. Beast! Scott Howell!)* Oh, hi!
   (What a lame-o.)

Him: Hi. Alex, right?

Me again: *(Don't say zit, don't say zit . . .)*
   I'm Alex. Reel. *(He knows your name,
   stupidhead!)*

Him: I know. We read together at the
   audition, remember?

Me: Oh, yeah. Sure. You're Scott Towel, right?
   *(Wrong! I want to die ten thousand deaths
   right on this spot . . .)*

Him: Actually, Scott Howell. With an H.

Me: *(Blubber, blubber . . . Say something.
   Anything!)* Hamlet, put a knife through
   me now.

Him: Don't worry. I get that a lot.

Me: *(Choking.)* Excuse me?

Him: The paper towel thing.

Me: *(First the zit, now this. He'll never speak to me again.)* I'm sorry. It's just, see, my sisters—never mind. So, have you acted a lot? (Better. Much better.)*

Him: Ever since I was a pumpkin in my second-grade Thanksgiving play. *(Laughter here.)*

Me: Don't feel too bad. I was a mushroom in kindergarten! No joke.

Him: So, you're really into acting, huh? I hear your mom and dad act at the Raven and everything. Pretty cool.

Me: Acting is the greatest. It's like, I don't know, a chance to forget everything. Be somebody else. *(Help! Do I sound stupid or intelligent?)*

Him: So, what's wrong with being you, Alex Reel?

Me: No, it's not that. . . . I just meant . . . Never mind.

Him: Is it like one minute you're you, this seventh-grader with homework and parents and a little sister who bugs you—

Me: *Two* little sisters!

Him: *(Laughing.)*—and the next minute, you're saying stuff that was just words on a page a second ago, but suddenly you believe it?

Me: Exactly. Wow! That's exactly it. The director calls "Curtain!" and there's a spot of light for you to stand in, and it's like you pick your character up off the floor and suddenly you're Anne Frank or Dorothy or . . .

Him: A mushroom?

Me: Yeah, I guess. *(Laughing.)*

Him: Well, I guess we won't know who got the parts till tomorrow, huh?

Me: You have to get Beast. You were so believable!

Him: Thanks, I think. It's a good thing to be good at being a big, ugly, hairy monster, right?

Me: Absolutely.

Him: Good luck.

Me: You too.

Him: See you tomorrow?

Alex in Love

Alex came home on cloud nine with flowers in her hair. No lie. She wore a braided crown of flowers (weeds, actually) around her head *in public* on the bus home and at the library and at the grocery store.

If you haven't guessed already, Alex got the part of Beauty—even without her lucky sweater.

I was dying to point this out, but then again I was afraid to bring it up. I thought, I hoped, she'd actually forgotten about the whole Sweater Incident for now, because she was so obsessed with:

A. Beauty (and the Beast)
B. Beauty (as in looks)
C. Paper Towel Man

D. Learning her lines (I'm supposed to help. Ha!)

E. Paper Towel Man (Did I say that already?)

Paper Towel Man got the part of Beast. Surprise, surprise.

He just called Alex *on the phone*. Joey answered and announced, "It's a boy!" for the whole world to hear, like a baby had just been born or something.

Alex didn't even get mad. (If I did that, she'd kill me!) She showed Joey and me his school picture. This Scott Towel was about as big as a pinhead, so what was I supposed to say?

Joey said he looked like a praying mantis! Ha!

OK. So, I'm not jumping-up-and-down, falling-over-thrilled for Alex the way Mom would be. Where's Mom when you need her?

All I know is, Mom'll make me help Alex with her lines, over and over and over. And in this house, plays always end up in a fight.

Alex says I just don't get the beauty of acting. I guess she's right. If you ask me, acting makes you sweat. Acting makes you want to throw up. Acting makes you afraid to fall. Take it from me.

I was onstage once, and only once.

I was a human piñata. No lie. I did not make this up. I am not exaggerating.

It was my first (and last!) time onstage.

Ask Joey. Ask Alex. Ask half the town of Acton. It was for Joey's birthday one time. Alex convinced me it would be fun to put on a play, and I wanted to be like my big sister, my mom, and my dad. But she did not tell me what the part was.

All I knew was I only had to remember one line: "Yum! Candy!" I knew I could do that. For days, I walked around the house, reciting, "Yum! Candy!" and rubbing my tummy like I was in a Campbell's Soup commercial or something.

What I didn't know was that I had to dress like Big Bird, get poked with a broomstick, and hang like a beehive in the wind.

The play was about this old washerwoman (Alex, of course) who comes into this house at night. She sees a piñata hanging there for the birthday party the next day. She knows the piñata is full of candy and can't resist trying some. So she gives the piñata— also known as *me*—a poke with her broom!

Dad strapped me into this contraption thingy, like a swing. It had all these straps so I could hang from the beam port, a big opening in the ceiling of the theater where more lights can hang.

It was so hot inside the bird that I could hardly breathe. I was pretty much gasping for air. And I remember hearing the little kids in the audience say, "Hey, I hear the piñata breathing!"

Anyway, whenever the washerwoman poked me, no candy was supposed to come out. But when she wasn't looking, I was supposed to say "Yum! Candy!" and throw down some candy to the kids.

That part was fun. At first . . .

But as soon as the kids started figuring out there was candy in there, they all ran up onstage and started jumping at me. They took Alex's broom, and she didn't even try to take it back! I threw down all the candy I had, but they kept poking me to try to get more. By this time, I was spinning around and around in circles. I was so dizzy, I couldn't feel my head. I was sure I'd throw up.

I yelled, "Stop! Let me down! Hey! Stop!" but the kids just kept jabbing and poking. Dad was operating the ropes from above. When he finally figured out what was going on, he tried to pull me up instead of lowering me into the sugar-crazed mob. The grand finale: my Big Bird costume got stuck going through the ceiling.

So, as you can see, being a human piñata was not exactly my ticket to stardom. See why I'm not in plays like the rest of the nuts (nut jobs!) around here?

BIOGRAPHY OF ALEX REEL, FAMOUS ACTRESS

Alex Reel is the firstborn child of the actress Susan Reel, who has acted for many years at the Raven, and former actor Richard Reel, whose famous roles include King Lear.

Alex has always been the light of their lives. Gifted since birth, Alex follows in the footsteps of generations of Reel actors to perform in such plays as *Mushroom in the Rain, The Fifth-Grade Nerd* (she was not the nerd), *Heidi,* and *The Sound of Music.* Her current role of Beauty in *Beauty and the Beast* is expected to take her to new heights on the way to stardom in an already stellar acting career.

POSSIBLE STAGE NAMES:
Alexis
Cricket Seagull
Alexandra Love Reel
Julia Trulove
Topaz

BLABBERMOUTH AND THE BEAST
Starring Alex

Me: *Knock, knock. (Making fake knocking noise by clicking tongue in doorway of sisters' room.)*

Me: *(To sisters.)* Sisters Club Meeting! Sisters Club Meeting!

Stevie: Now?

Joey: In here?

Me: Your room's bigger.

Stevie: Ha! It is not!

Me: C'mon, you guys. You're always saying we don't get to have fun anymore. This'll be fun. I promise.

Stevie: Like how?

Me: Like we're going to put on a play.

Joey: Yay!

Stevie: That's not a real Sisters Club thing. That's just a way to get *us* to help *you* practice your lines.

Joey: Who cares? C'mon, Stevie.

Stevie: Can't you just practice with Scott Towel? I don't feel like—

Me: You owe me. Don't make me say "thirty-dollar pot holder"!

Stevie: OK, OK.

Me: Good. It's all settled, then. I, the most beautiful sister, get to be Beauty. I will also be the director, of course.

Joey: You always get to boss everybody.

Me: It's *my* play. Stevie, you're Beast.

Stevie: I'm *Beast*? What do I do?

Me: First of all, you can't just say lines. Get into the character. Feel what it's like to be Beast.

Stevie: Feel what it's like to be all hairy and ugly?

Me: You know what I mean. Here, put a fuzzy blanket around you. It will help you feel more Beast-y. Joey, you're the narrator.

Joey: Can't I be Chip the Teacup, like in the movie?

Me: You're going to be Joey the Broken Cup if you don't stop arguing. You're our stand-in if we need a tree or a horse, too.

Joey: A tree and a horse don't even talk!

Me: Then do sound effects. OK, everybody. Quiet on the set. Joey, start reading here. Action!

Joey: "Once there was a merchant who was very rich. He had three daughters. The youngest was not only prettier than her sisters, but the nicest."

Stevie: Hey! You're making that up.

Joey: Nah-uh. Look. It says right here.

Me: OK, blah blah. Let's say all Beauty asked for was a rose. When the dad picks one of Beast's roses, Beast says the father must die unless he gives him his daughter.

Joey: Hey! You just took my whole part.

Me: Never mind that. Let's take up where Beauty first comes to stay with Beast. Stevie, upstage left.

Stevie: Huh?

Me: It's blocking. Forget it. Just stand over by the window. *(Joey taps yogurt containers against desk for horse galloping.)*

Stevie: "Tell me now, do you not consider me very ugly?"

Me: "I do, since I cannot but speak the truth. But I also find you very kind."

Stevie: "Alas, in addition to being ugly, I'm afraid I'm also dim-witted. I am a mere beast."

Me: Say it like you mean it. And don't just look out the window. Mr. Cannon says, "Respond to your fellow actors."

Stevie: Is Mr. Cannon this bossy?

Me: Stand like this, with your legs bent. Arm out. Mr. Cannon says keep your character in your head, but let your body tell the story.

Stevie: Does Mr. Cannon say this play should be called *Blabbermouth and the Beast*?

Me: *(Ignoring her.)* "Nonsense. A dim-witted person would not admit it so. Besides, you have a kind heart. When I think of that, you are no longer ugly."

Stevie: "Beauty, will you be my wife?" *(Laughing.)*

Me: C'mon, Stevie. You can't just crack up.

Joey: Oh, Beauty, my Beauty. Kiss me,
O Beauteous One. You know you want to.
Mww, mww, mww. (Makes kissing sounds.)
I'm not really an ugly Beast. I'm Scott
Towel. *Mww, mww.*

Me: Joey! We don't need sound effects for
kissing!

Stevie: Hey, just so you know, I'm not going
to kiss you or anything, if that's what
you think.

Me: Stop acting like babies, you guys. This
is *acting*.

Stevie: I'm still not kissing you.

Joey: Here, kiss this. *(Shows roll of paper
towels.)*

Stevie: Great idea, Joey. Paper towels can be
Beast.

Joey: The paper towels can be Scott Towel.
Get it?

Me: I'm not kissing a roll of paper towels.

Stevie: Go with it, Alex. *Feel* the part.

Joey: Maybe this'll help. *(Draws face on
paper towels.)*

Stevie: Perfect! *(Holds paper-towel Beast out toward Beauty.)* "Beauty, will you be my wife?"

Me: *(Kissing paper towels.)* Mww! Mww! Goodbye, Dear Beast. I shall miss you so.

Stevie: I can't believe you actually did it.

Joey: Ha, ha, ha, ha, ha! Alex kissed paper towels!

Me: You guys have paper towels on the brain. Rule Number One in acting is don't be afraid to look stupid.

Stevie: You sure got that rule down. *(Stevie and Joey fall on the floor, laughing.)*

Me: You guys don't know anything—about acting or boys or kissing.

Joey: We know one thing. Alex is in love with a paper towel! *(Falls on floor, laughing some more.)*

Scott Howell
Scott
SCOTT
S + A
Scott Howell
Scott
SCOTT HOWELL
Scott Howell
Scott Howell
Scott Howell

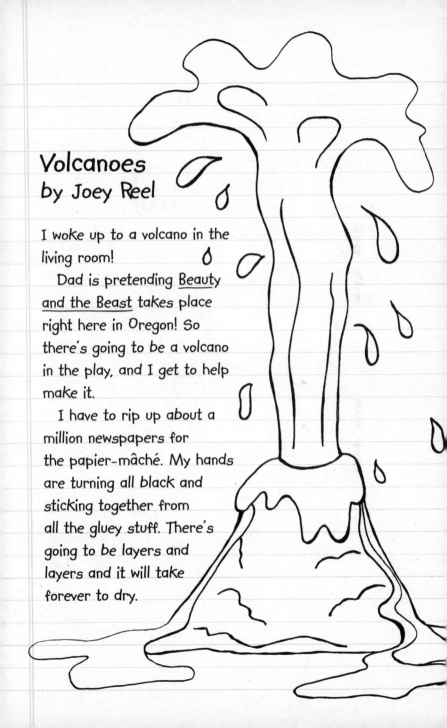

Volcanoes
by Joey Reel

I woke up to a volcano in the living room!

Dad is pretending <u>Beauty and the Beast</u> takes place right here in Oregon! So there's going to be a volcano in the play, and I get to help make it.

I have to rip up about a million newspapers for the papier-mâché. My hands are turning all black and sticking together from all the gluey stuff. There's going to be layers and layers and it will take forever to dry.

At least ripping up newspapers is better than acting—no kissing!

Things OK to Kiss:

- Dad
- Hedgie
- School paper that gets an A

Things I will never, ever, not-ever kiss:
- A praying mantis
- A paper towel
- A boy (that looks like a praying mantis or a paper towel)

Guess Who's Coming to Dinner?

Alex put on The Hat at Family Dinner one night. I'd been cooking a lot lately, and Family Dinner (Tacos à la Stevie, minus any ears) was actually edible now.

"OK, I have something to say—an important announcement."

"Sounds serious," said Dad, tapping his spoon on a glass to get everybody's attention.

"What is it?" asked Mom.

"The play is only one week away, and we still don't know our lines. So I asked Scott, the guy who plays Beast, to come over and practice with me."

"Scott *Towel*?" asked Joey.

"Puh! That's your big announcement?" I asked, like *Do I care?*

"I just want Joey and Stevie to promise they won't embarrass me."

"What about Mom and Dad?" I asked.

"Ha, ha," said Dad.

"I mean it, you guys. No calling him Scott Towel and stuff."

"I promise!" said Joey.

"I don't!" I said.

"I think you should ask him to stay for dinner," said Dad. "We'd like to get to know this boy a bit if you're going to be spending time together."

"Good idea," Mom chimed in. "I won't be home after school, and I'd like to meet him, too."

"Aw, do I really have to?" Alex asked. "It's so embarrassing!"

"We think it's a good idea, too," I chimed in, getting Joey to nod her head in agreement. "He should meet the whole family."

"Alex's boyfriend is coming to dinner!" Joey said, teasing.

"First of all, Joey, and everybody, he is NOT my boyfriend. Second of all, if you embarrass me, I promise you will end up like the sisters in *Beauty and the Beast*—turned to stone!" Alex gave Joey and me an evil, squinty-eyed look.

"Since your *boy*friend's coming over, does this mean I don't have to play Beast anymore?" I asked. "If I have to say 'I'll die of hunger without your beauty' once more, I think I'll throw up."

"Hmm. I'll have to think of something special to make," Mom said.

"But Mom, you'll be tired of cooking, won't you?" said Alex. "I mean, after cooking on the show all day?"

"You want Stevie to cook, don't you?" Mom asked.

Alex nodded. "Well, that's a relief," said Mom.

It made me feel appreciated, for once. "I'll think of something," I said.

"Anything but Macaroni Disaster," said Alex.

"OK. But it'll cost you."

"Beast!" said Alex, just like old times.

Everybody tried to act normal, like Alex was just having a friend over, no big deal. But really, you could tell everybody was holding their breath for the big night, all because it was A BOY.

I don't get what the big deal is about boys. I mean, they have huge feet and their ears stick out. They snort in class and make armpit noises and call girls names like Maggot and Pootney. It's not like some prince was coming to dinner. (Well, maybe the FROG prince.) After all, the kid *was* a Beast.

I thought about trying to make something special. Really I did. After all, I still felt kind of bad about the Sweater Pot Holder.

Then I had a brainstorm. A brilliant, boy-coming-to-dinner brainstorm.

I saw it on Mom's show. Fondue Sue did a whole episode on fondue—the dinner you melt in a pot! You get these long forks and dip stuff like bread or strawberries into cheese or chocolate. It even has funny names like Chocolate Cherry Fun-due.

Fondue was perfect for the big dinner:

1. It's French. (Alex would be all over that.)
2. How hard could it be to melt stuff?
3. If you drop fondue in the pot, something funny happens! (I can't wait to tell Joey!)

Rules for Boys Coming to Dinner
by Joey Reel

Do:

- Remember NOT to call him Scott Towel (right!).
- Set the table with <u>paper</u> <u>towels</u> for napkins.
- Wear nice clothes (maybe even pioneer dress?).
- Bump the boy to make his fondue fall off the fork!

Don't:

- Bring up Sock Monkey.
- Show baby pictures of Alex.
- Let Dad tell embarrassing stories about the old days.
- Use the word <u>boyfriend</u> (unless you want to turn into a statue).

Do:

- Tell funny jokes!

Q: Who is Scott Towel's brother?
A: Scott Tissue (a.k.a. toilet paper!).

Q: Who is Scott Towel's cousin?
A: Scotch Tape!

FONDUES AND FON-DON'TS
Starring Alex

Me: *(Entering with the Boy and looking at all the bowls on the table.)* Wait! Stevie? What's this? We're having croutons for dinner? *(Not another Macaroni Disaster!)*

Joey: Not just croutons. There's cheese glop, too.

Stevie: *Fon-due.* It's French.

Me: French? Of course! We're eating French tonight. Yum! French cheese glop.

Scott: Should I sit . . . where?

Stevie and Joey: *(At the same time.)* THERE! Next to Alex.

Joey: And me!

Dad: Fondue is French for "to melt."

Joey: I thought it was French for "to kiss." *(I try to turn Joey to stone with my thought waves.)*

Mom: *(Trying to save the day.)* Mmm. Look at this cheese and bubbly tomato sauce and chocolate for dessert. Where did you learn to make all this?

Stevie: Mo-om. I saw it on *your* show.

Me: *(To Scott.)* Um, my mom has a cooking show on TV.

Scott: Oh, yeah. My mom said she watches you, Mrs. Reel. *(Scott looks at Stevie.)* So you made all this? Looks . . . interesting.

Stevie: Thanks a lot.

Mom: Stevie, why don't you tell Scott, and us, how this works?

Stevie: OK, you pick up one of these long forks. Then you get bread or a marshmallow or fruit, stab it with your fork, and dip it into one of the sauces.

Me: What are they?

Stevie: There's Cheese Fiesta Fondue and Pizza Fondue. This I call Chocolate Meltdown, and that one's Yin-Yang.

Joey: Yin-Yang?

Stevie: Chocolate and Marshmallow.

Joey: Those aren't *toe* marshmallows, are they?

Me: *(Oh, no!)* Joey, shhh! *(Please, please, please don't let anybody ask what toe marshmallows are!)*

Stevie: I made sure to use marshmallows that Alex didn't put between her toes.

Me: *(Can't they keep quiet about anything?)* *(To Scott.)* Just ignore them.

Stevie: Eat the regular stuff first. Like the bread and vegetables. Then you get *non-toe* marshmallows for dessert. Or orange slices to dip in the chocolate.

Me: *(With a glare.)* I hope that's the only orange thing tonight.

Joey: And guess what? *(Looks at Scott.)* If you drop your food in the cheese, you have to kiss all the girls at the table!

Me: Joey! *(What are those two up to? I'm going to kill them later!)*

Scott: Um, she's not serious, is she?

Stevie: That's the rule!

Me: You guys! *(To Scott.)* Aren't little sisters really annoying?

Scott: *(Nodding.)* I know.

Joey: Does your sister call you Scott Towel?

Me: JO-EY! *(Alex Reel, promising young*

actress, found dead of embarrassment at
the dinner table last evening. . . .)

Joey: I didn't make it up, you know.
About dropping your fondue and kissing
all the girls. Stevie learned it on
Mom's show.

Mom: It's true. *(Not Mom, too!)* It's an honest-
to-goodness custom that goes with eating
fondue. Remember, honey?

Dad: Boy, do I.

Me: Then you had me and lived happily ever
after. OK, can we please talk about
something else now?

Stevie: Does anybody need a *paper towel*—
I mean napkin?

Mom: Why do we have paper towels for
napkins? There should be blue napkins in
the cupboard, Stevie. *(Joey and Stevie*
burst out laughing.)

Joey: I set the table. I really think we need
paper towels. Good thing I put out *paper*
towels for napkins, huh, Stevie? *(Scott*
turns bright red.)

Me: Jo-ey! *(Boy is she gonna hear from me later!) (To Scott.)* See what I mean? Sisters are the worst.

Scott: *(Covers mouth with hand and coughs.)*

Stevie: At least we don't go around kissing paper towels, right, Joey? *(I'll never be able to look him in the eye again!)*

Joey: And talking to a sock monkey like it's a person.

Me: *(OK, that's it. I'm gonna wrap my sisters up and send them air mail to the moon!)* You guys! Mom, Dad, may they please be excused?

Joey: I'm not done yet. I only had one crouton. One crouton is not dinner.

Stevie: I made this whole dinner. I don't want to be excused.

Dad: Girls. How about . . . Let's talk about the play. Have you two seen the rose garden I'm making for the outside of Beast's castle? Each flower is handcrafted out of tissue paper.

Me: That's cool, Dad.

Dad: Scott, tell us about playing Beast. What's it like? Do you have your costume finished?

Joey: Are you going to be really, really hairy? *(Joey bumps Scott's arm for like the tenth time.)*

Me: JO-EY!

Fascinating Fondue Factoids
by Joey Reel

Fondue comes from the French word <u>fondre</u>, which means "to melt."

Most popular fondue: cheese.

Fondue started in Switzerland, as a way of using up all the old cheese that had turned hard.

Don't throw away the golden crust left on the bottom of the fondue pot. . . . It's the best part!

It's a tradition. . . . If a woman or girl drops the fondue from her fork, she has to kiss all the men or boys at the table.

If a boy or man drops his fondue into the pot, he has to kiss all the women or girls.

The world's largest fondue weighed 2,100 pounds. It was made from 1,190 pounds of grated Gruyère cheese from Wisconsin. After the fondue was measured for the world record, the cheese was donated to a food rescue organization in New York City.

Stevie's Secret Family Recipes:

Pizza Fondue

1 package cheddar cheese, cut into cubes
2 cups shredded mozzarella
1 jar tomato sauce
1 loaf Italian bread for dipping

Hey, now it's not a secret anymore! ~S

Mix cheeses and heat until melted. Stir in tomato sauce until smooth. Dip bread cubes, mushrooms, or green pepper slices into mixture.

Serious (Chocolate) Meltdown

12 oz. semisweet chocolate
1 cup half-and-half
1 tsp. vanilla

Break chocolate bar into pieces. (Chocolate chips work too, but they're not as much fun.) Put all the pieces into a pan and add the half-and-half. Turn heat on low and stir until smooth. Add vanilla at the end.

CHOCO BAR

DO dip in chocolate fondue:

- Apples
- Strawberries
- Bananas
- Pineapple
- Pound cake
- Marshmallows

DON'T dip in the fondue:

- LEGOs
- Dominoes
- Fingers (germs—yuck!)

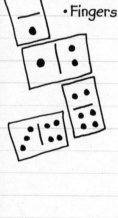

Frog Lips!

All during dinner, I kept looking at Alex, who was looking at Scott Towel like she was all gaga in love—like she actually *wanted* him to drop his fondue! I mean, what are the chances you'll actually marry the person whose name you write over and over a hundred times in your seventh-grade notebook?

Zero to none.

Gaga Alex didn't seem at all like the sister who used to come to Sisters Club Meetings.

"Stevie?" Alex asked. "Are you actually going to eat that? Or just hold it there for a year? You're causing a traffic jam, you know."

"I'm concentrating," I told her (on not dropping my

119

fondue so I won't have to kiss anybody!). I dipped my zucchini carefully into the fondue pot. The plan was for Scott Towel to drop his fondue, NOT me.

Dad cracked one of his really bad jokes. "Honey," said Dad, in front of everybody, even the Boy. "I just want you to know, I'm so fon-due you!" Like "fond of" you. Get it? Ha, ha, ha. Dad must be from the Planet Cardigan, like those grandpa sweaters Mr. Rogers wears. We're talking *Old School*.

Mom actually thought it was funny. Alex had a look on her face like she wanted to crawl under the table and disappear.

"Ee-uw! Dad! You made me dip my zucchini in chocolate!" I said.

The Boy spoke. "This is all good," he said.

"For melty, lumpy cheese glop, you mean," said Joey.

"This tastes much better than the fondue I made on TV," said Mom.

"Stevie, you're getting to be quite the cook," said Dad. "Good for you."

"Good for *us*," said Alex. Everybody laughed, even Mom.

I think they actually liked the fondue. Even Alex said it was way better than Chinese takeout. I couldn't help it, though—I kept half-expecting to find a rubber ear à la Joey floating in the cheese glop.

I guess she was too busy with her Bump-into-Scott routine. We planned it that Joey would sit next to Scott Towel. Even better, it turns out he's left-handed and Joey's right-handed. "Like normal people and NON-boys," Joey pointed out. So it was perfect for bumping elbows.

"If you're left-handed, it means you're creative," said Alex. "An artist."

"I think it just means you bump into stuff more," said Joey. "See?" She bumped Scott's elbow, trying to get him to drop his fondue off the fork.

After that, every time Scott Towel (a.k.a. Scotch Tape) reached for the fondue, Joey went *BUMP!*

The Boy scooched his chair closer to Alex.

As soon as Mom and Dad weren't looking, Joey bumped his elbow again, then played innocent. Still nothing happened.

The Boy gave Joey a "Cut it out" look, but he didn't say it out loud. He just took a sip of water.

I tried to signal Joey, to make my eyes say, "It's not working! Do it again!"

That's when it happened.

The Boy had a hunk of bread on the end of his fork. He dipped it in the cheese and started to lift it out. He waited for a second while the cheese went *drip, drip, drip*, and just at that exact moment, I saw Joey go in for the kill.

BUMP!

His cheesy bread slipped and fell and landed— *PLOP!*—right smack-dab in the middle of the cheesy cheese.

I looked at Joey. Joey looked at me.

Scott Towel was still chasing his cheese lump around the pot, hoping he wouldn't get caught.

"LOOK!" shouted Joey, pointing to the lump in the pot.

"Empty fork!" I shouted. "Empty fork!"

"Uh-oh. Bad news," said Dad. "Looks to me like he dropped it."

"I didn't—really it was—she bumped me!" He pulled his fork out of the fondue pot and knocked over his glass of water.

"Sorry. I didn't mean to . . ."

"It's OK," Mom said, handing him paper-towel napkins to sop up all the dripping water.

"Alex first!" Joey shouted. "Kiss Alex first!"

Scott Towel turned tomato-red, worse than Pizza Fondue. He pretended to wipe up some more water drips and disappeared under the table. Nobody knew what to do. Alex looked like she might cry. Joey pushed back the tablecloth to see what he was doing under there.

Finally, Scott pulled his head out from under the table. On the way back up, he accidentally bumped into Joey's ear—with his lips!

Everybody was silent. Like the whole family had turned to stone.

"Bluck! Frog lips!" Joey yelled. She actually said *frog lips*! No lie. Then she got up from the table and ran to our room.

Without dessert.

Bluck!
(A poem by Joey Reel)

Boys are blucky and yucky.
Leftie!
Ucky, too.
Cooties!
Kissed by a praying mantis!

Volcano Alex

I, Middle Sister, Glue Girl, ran after her.

I had to make sure Joey was OK (not to mention saving my *own* life). After all, neither of us *ever* thought this would end up with Joey getting a big, wet, boy ear-smooch.

"Open up!" I banged on the door to our room. Nothing.

I looked down the hall, at the stairs, trying to think of how to get Joey to open the door before Alex caught up with us. "Hey, Joey! Let me in! Hurry up, before Frog Lips plants a wet one on me."

Click! Joey opened the door.

"Phew, that was close," I said to Joey.

"It's too late for me," Joey said, still swiping at her ear with her sleeve.

"Just think of it like . . . a doggie slurp," I suggested.

"Ye-ah. A *Scotty* dog!" She gave her ear one last swipe, then went back to scribbling in that notebook of hers.

"Look what I'm making!" She held up a NO KISSING sign. A pair of lips with a big red circle and stripe through it.

Against my better instincts, we laughed ourselves silly just thinking about the look on Scott Towel's face.

"Maybe I should draw an ear with a red line through it, too," Joey said.

I cackled some more, to cover up for feeling guilty about starting the whole Fondue Freak Show.

All of a sudden, we heard *Wham! Wham! Wham!* on the door. Definitely Alex. It was her "You better open the door" knock.

"Nobody's home!" Joey called.

"Let me in!" yelled Alex.

"Not by the hair of our chinny-chin-chins!" I called. That got Joey giggling all over again.

Alex burst in. "You guys are *so* not funny!" Alex said.

"I ask you to be nice and you go and ruin everything, you . . . you . . . purple-hued maltworms!"

"What did we do?" I asked innocently. Like I didn't know.

"You two embarrassed me big-time in front of my friend. He looked like he wet his pants, 'cause you made him spill that water . . ."

"Scott Towel wet his pants!" Joey said. I bit my cheeks to keep from laughing.

"And now Dad's taking him home, and we didn't even get to practice the play or anything."

"At least *you* didn't have to practice kissing!" said Joey.

"I hate you!" said Alex. "I hate you both! I don't care what anybody says about sisters. I'm never speaking to you again. Ever."

I knew Alex was mad—but I didn't know Volcano Alex was about to erupt. I mean, really explode.

"I quit!" Alex shouted at us. "Do you hear me? I quit the Sisters Club! Forever and ever!"

Dear Sock Monkey:
My older sister is mad at me, so she's giving me the Silent Treatment. What can I do to make her talk to me again? And don't you give me the Silent Treatment, too!
~ Freezing in My Own Family (a.k.a. Stevie)

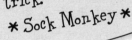

Dear Freezing:
Hmm. Hard question. Let her know you're sorry. Think of a special way to make it up to her. Give it time. Breakfast in bed helps. Blueberry pancakes with whipped cream just might do the trick.

* Sock Monkey *

128

The Silent Treatment

Since Alex wouldn't talk to me, I thought I'd listen in on her talking to Sock Monkey. As in *spy*. I was lying on the floor (under the bed) where I could hear most of what she was saying through the old iron grate, where the heat comes through.

"Are you living under the bed now?" asked Joey.

"Shhh! Can't you see I'm eavesdropping?"

"On who?"

"Alex and Sock Monkey!"

"What are they saying?"

"Mostly just *Beauty and the Beast* stuff. Stuff about us, too!"

"What stuff?"

"The usual. Evil wicked stepsister stuff."

"She's really mad this time, huh?" said Joey.

"Volcano mad!" I said. "But at least volcanoes only erupt every two thousand years."

"What's wrong with her, anyway? Why's she acting funny like this?"

"Mom says maybe it's hormones. Dad says it's a midlife crisis, between being a kid and a teenager. Maybe it's a mid-*love* crisis! I just heard her say she *wanted* Scott Towel to kiss her!"

"No way!"

"Way!"

"I wish she would talk to us," Joey said. "Do stuff, like we used to."

"Me too, Duck."

"And stop thinking we're purple mealworms."

"Purple-hued maltworms?"

"Whatever."

"Is she really quitting the Sisters Club, you think?"

"You can't quit your sisters, Duck. Sisters are forever. Remember?"

"I miss Alex and the Sisters Club. I even miss her bossing us."

I didn't say anything. But the real truth, the whole

truth, and nothing but the truth was that I missed my sister, too. She could have been talking to me, whispering secrets to me. Instead, she was spilling her guts to a stupid old pair of socks with eyes. Telling it she *wanted* to get kissed. By a B-O-Y! I just didn't get it.

"Hello? Earth to Stevie."

"I know, I know. You want to show me something."

I slid out from under the bed. Joey cracked up. "You should see you. You have dust bunnies all over your hair!"

"And I found a LEGO fairy, two quarters, and the silver locket from your pioneer doll."

"Hey! I've been looking everywhere for those! By the way, I lost two quarters."

"Did not!"

"Did, too!"

I handed Joey the locket and the LEGO and put the quarters in my pocket.

"Are you coming or not?"

"Not."

"C'mon, Stevie. Please? You have to."

I followed Joey downstairs. One sister mad at me was enough.

Joey had been helping Dad paint the volcano. She took me by the hand and led me around to the back of the volcano. "Look! Look what I did! It's so funny!"

I crouched down on my knees and saw where Joey had painted initials with a big red heart around them.

"Joey, are you nuts? That's not funny. Alex is mad enough at us already!"

Joey stuck out her pout-face lip. "Well, I think it's funny. Besides, who's going to see it? It's in the bottom corner."

"I'm telling you. You better paint over it if you ever want your big sister to speak to you again."

Sisters
(a poem by Joey Reel)

So mean
Icky
So bossy
Talk to sock monkeys, not you
Extremely bad friends
Really not nice
Silent Treatment

(I helped with that one.)
~S

Divorce, Sisters Style

It felt terrible to be in a house full of silence.
I'd been in Alex's House of Bad Moods before, but this
was different. Like a rubber band that you stretch too
far and it snaps. Like a bowl you break by mistake,
and it stares up at you in pieces.

Ever since Mom got her show and Alex got into the
play, something had changed. Something felt broken,
worse than a sweater that unraveled or a dinner that
went haywire.

Like our whole family was coming apart.

I decided it was up to me to fix it, to make things
right with Alex again. After all, I'm the middle sister.
I'm the glue, right?

Middles are the peacemakers. I read that in a magazine article once. A real, actual magazine article. Not like the ones Alex is always quoting and pretending she read somewhere.

I remember it said firstborns may be smarter, and last-borns may be shorter, but middles are more likely to live the "exhilarating life" of an artist or adventurer. (Cool!) It named a bunch of other jobs, too. I don't remember them all, but I remember it ended with firefighter.

So . . . looks like it's time for me to go put out some fires.

firstborn

★ **Are you bossy?** (Like Alex.)
★ **Do you like to be in charge?** (Like Alex thinks she is.)
★ **Do you have big ideas and big plans?**
★ **Do you hear yourself saying,**
   "Why can't I get away with anything?"

→ **You may be the oldest**
   in your family.

- -

Some other qualities of the firstborn are:

- Confident
- Determined
- Super-organized (I don't think so!)
- Eager to please (If only.)
- Responsible (Ha!)
- Emotionally intense, dramatic (They sure know Alex.)
- Perfectionist
- Ambitious
- Born leader make
- Likes to ~~avoid~~ trouble
- Famous firstborns include astronaut Sally Ride, Jimmy Carter, and Oprah Winfrey.

ORDER QUIZ!

middle

★ Are you often in a good mood?
★ Do you like to step in to settle arguments?
★ Are you good at fighting injustice?
★ Do you ever feel stuck in the middle?
★ Do you hear yourself saying,
  "Nobody ever listens to me?"

→ **You may be the middle child in your family.**

Some other qualities of the middle child are:

- Lots of loyal friends (a.k.a. my best friend, Olivia)
- Good at keeping secrets (That's me!)
- Peacemaker (Oh, yeah.)
- Concerned about the needs of others
- Creative (They should make a candy heart for this.)
- Independent
- Flexible and adaptable
- Sees both sides of an issue (I'm cool.)
- Famous middles include Madonna, Susan B. Anthony, and Martin Luther King, Jr.
- Feels like a sandwich (They left an important one out!)

continued on next page→

QUIZ

youngest

★ **Do you like to be the center of attention?** (Joey)
★ **Do you always like to get your way?** (Joey)
★ **Do you make friends easily?**
★ **Do you go out of your way to be unique?**
★ **Do you hear yourself saying,**
  "Everybody treats me like a baby!" (Joey all the way!)

→ **You may be the youngest child in your family.**

Some other qualities of the youngest child are:

- Funny, comical, makes people laugh
- Good at acting (Don't tell Alex!)
- Great storyteller
- Spoiled (No way!)   ← (Hey, Joey wrote those!)
- Likes to break the rules (Who, me?)
- Affectionate (No Frog Lips, please.)
- Makes friends easily
- Laid-back, easygoing
- Creative, unconventional
- Doesn't give up easily
- Famous youngests include Joan of Arc, Bill Gates, and Copernicus.

★ If you're an only child, you get to be first, middle, and youngest child, all in one.
★ Onlies have some qualities of all the others.
★ Do you find yourself saying, "If only I had a sister or a brother"?

→ **You may be the only child in your family.**

Some other qualities of an "only" are:
- Good at making decisions
- Confident
- Good at expressing opinions
- Pays attention to detail
- Always on time
- Good in school
- Likes to read
- Good at math
- Does not like to share
- Likes to be first
- Critical of self and others   ← (He's funny!)
- Famous onlies include Robin Williams, Franklin D. Roosevelt, (Famous president) and Sarah Michelle Gellar.
   (Who's that?)

I would have to pull a Martin Luther King, Jr., on my family. Only one problem—Alex still wasn't speaking to me. So I had to start by getting her to talk.

I waited till Saturday. I woke up early, before Joey or Alex. I went downstairs and made Alex her favorite breakfast. Then I carried it up to her room on a tray, like Mom used to do when we were sick.

I knocked on Alex's door. "Alex! Wake up!"

No answer.

"I made you breakfast," I said. "Your favorite!"

"Blueberry pancakes?" She spoke! It was a start.

"No."

"French toast with blueberries?"

"No."

"Blueberry anything?"

"Blueberry waffles!" I said. "With warmed-up maple syrup."

"Just leave it outside the door."

"I can't."

"Why not?"

"It's breakfast IN BED. It's no fair if you have to get out of bed."

"And who do you think's going to open the door? Sock Monkey?"

"C'mon, Alex. Let me in."

"But I'm not talking to you."

"You just did."

"That was a fluke."

Miracle of miracles, the door opened. Alex stuck Sock Monkey through the crack and made him say, "You can bring Alex the breakfast, but that's all."

I pushed open the door.

"Alex, you can't stay mad at me forever, you know."

"Yes, she can," said Sock Monkey.

"But I can't stand it if you're mad at me for like the rest of my life. I can't stand it if you don't want to be my sister. C'mon, Alex. I said I'm sorry like a million times."

"Alex said to tell you a million and one times is not enough for what you did," said Sock Monkey.

"Well, then, how can I make it up to you? I mean her. I mean . . . I made you breakfast. And I did the dishes for you, and I didn't tell Dad it was you who flooded the bathroom."

"Alex said to tell you she *so* did not flood the bathroom!" said Sock Monkey.

"Well, there was a lake on the floor, and Dad was mad, and Alex was the last one in there."

141

"Stop changing the subject," said Sock Monkey. "Alex is the one mad at you, remember?"

"How can I forget? You won't talk to us, and it's making Joey cry. Just tell me what to do. Anything. I'll kiss Sock Monkey. See? *Mww.*" I kissed that worn old bag of stuffing right on his ruby-red sock lips. "I'll kiss paper towels if you want me to!"

Even Alex could not hold back a smile.

"OK. I'll speak to you and Joey again," said Alex the Person. "But that's all. This doesn't mean I'm your friend. This doesn't mean I'm back in the Sisters Club. It's not over, you know. You owe me. And you better make it up to me."

"How?"

"You'll think of something."

Break a Leg!

Opening night. That's the biggest night of the play.

Everybody was backstage, buzzing around like bees, rushing around half-dressed, pacing back and forth, and holding scripts and mouthing lines to themselves. Mr. Cannon, the director, was racing around with a clipboard, shouting orders at people. Actors kept coming up to him, saying stuff like "I can't find the rose for the rosebush" or "Am I supposed to come onstage before or after the word 'night?'" or "My hair won't stay on right."

Even I couldn't help catching a little of the excitement.

Joey was trying to make up for the Frog Lips Incident, so she yelled, "Hi, Scott Towel!" to Scott (a.k.a. Beast), who was only half-hairy so far (from the neck down) and kept putting breath-mint strips in his mouth.

Alex was talking a mile a minute. Every few seconds she'd stop and blow into her hand, taking a bunch of deep breaths. She sounded like a hyperventilating hyena. She looked like she was going to throw up on Dad's shoes.

Dad said, "Alex, honey. Try to stay calm. Turn your nervousness into excitement. Remember your deep breathing? Now's the time. Breathe. Don't forget, if you blank on a line or say the wrong words, just keep going."

"I know, I know, Dad. The show must go on."

"That's my girl. I'll be backstage checking on my props and scene changes, if you need me."

"You look beautiful, honey," Mom said, and she gave Alex a non–Frog Lips kiss.

"Mom! I don't even have the rest of my costume on yet. And you're messing up my stage makeup."

"OK, well, you still look beautiful."

"Dad, did you remember the moat around the castle?" Joey asked.

"It's all there, honey."

"And are you sure you got the volcano in the right place? Facing the right way and everything?" It was just a hunk of cardboard and wire and paste, but you'd think Joey had helped build the Golden Gate Bridge or something.

"Five minutes!" Mr. Cannon called.

"Thank you—five!" a bunch of cast members called back.

Five minutes till showtime. Time to find our seats.

"Good luck!" I called to Alex.

Alex turned around with a mean glare. "Stevie! Don't say that. Good luck is like bad luck in acting!"

"Whatever."

"Take it back!"

"OK, OK! I take it back."

"Break a leg!" Joey called.

The best part about plays is sitting in the dark. You have hundreds of people around you, but the dark makes it seem like it's just you. Alone. You and the play. You get to laugh and cry and feel stuff and forget everything else, like homework, and fondue fiascoes, and sisters being mad at you.

Being in the audience is the best. You're inside the story, only you don't have to be up there acting.

Nervous. Shaky. Sweating.

Feeling like you're about to throw up.

If only Joey would stop whispering all the lines. I had to keep elbowing her, fondue-style. Once I even made her drop her Junior Mints.

Alex didn't seem one bit nervous. She didn't sound like a hyena anymore. Of course, you can't see the somersaults going on inside a person's stomach. But she didn't mess up one time in all of Act One.

Not even when I hunched down, crept down to the pit in front, and snapped a bunch of pictures of her.

Not even when the curtain got stuck.

Not even when Beast's nose fell off one time!

She did all the stuff Dad was always telling her— like when to look at the audience and how to speak loud enough and all that junk. I don't know how she keeps it all in her head.

And she looked just like Beauty in the fairy tale.

146

Not like someone who slams doors, throws herself facedown on her bed, and talks to a sock monkey. Not like someone who swears in Shakespeare or gives you the Silent Treatment or puts marshmallows between her toes.

I tried to think of myself in that dress. To imagine what it would be like. Picture it. It was a big step up from Human Piñata, that's for sure. I wondered if the dress and the makeup help transform you, I mean, make you feel like you're somebody besides yourself.

I got so caught up in the story and costumes and characters, the first act went by in a flash. Before I knew it, the curtain fell with a hush, and we could hear the patter of feet as the scenery changed.

BEAUTY AND THE BEAST, ACT TWO
Starring Alex
SETTING: THE HOUSE OF BEAUTY'S FATHER.

Beauty: *(Bursts into tears.)* *(Real tears! This is good!)*

Beauty's sister: Beauty? Whatever is wrong that causes you to weep so?

Beauty: I've had a most frightful dream this night. I was in the palace garden, and a lady appeared to me. She showed me Beast, lying on the grass, nearly dead. My poor, dear Beast! I fear I've made a most dreadful mistake. *(I haven't forgotten one line so far!)*

Sister: Nonsense. You belong here with us, with Father.

Beauty: I fear I am indeed very wicked to cause my poor, dear Beast so much grief. He has shown me nothing but kindness. Why did I not wish to marry him? *(Act Two is almost over—they love me!)*

Sister: Marry him! Have you lost your senses?

Beauty: Is it his fault that he is so ugly and has so few wits? *(Yes! I didn't say "zits!")*

Sister: Perhaps not . . .

Beauty: Why did I not wish to marry him? It is neither good looks nor brains in a husband that make a woman happy. It is beauty of character, goodness, and kindness. *(This is the best play ever! I'm a star!)*

Sister: Certainly you would not be so foolish as to think yourself in love with the Beast?

Beauty: Yes, and to prove my love, I shall remove this ring. *(I hope I can get it off!)* Soon I shall find myself back at the palace of my beloved, where I belong.

Sister: NO!

Beauty: Alas! 'Tis too late, my dear sister. Good-bye! *(I wish this scene wasn't over! Maybe if I ad-lib. Add just a line . . .)*

Beauty: *(Holding hand to head.)* Beast, O my dear, sweet Beast. Where art thou? *(Runs around stage, looking here and there. Exits by the volcano.)* Oops! *(Tripping.)*

CRASH! (Audience gasps.)

Beauty: "Curtain! Curtain!"

Curtain falls on Act Two.

Kissing Paper Towels

Just when I was starting to think that maybe acting wasn't so bad after all.

When the house lights came up at intermission, Mom and Joey and I ran backstage to check on Alex. The girl who played one of Beauty's sisters in the play came rushing up to us.

"Mrs. Reel—you gotta come—now," she said, all out of breath. "Alex! Her foot—it's bad—all swelled up like a baseball."

Mom pushed through the crowd and ran up the stage steps, with Joey and me right behind her.

Alex was propped up against a wall, her leg sticking out. Dad was holding an ice pack to her ankle. Mr. Cannon and a bunch of the cast were swarming around her. Her makeup was all runny, and her dress looked like a deflated birthday-party balloon.

Everybody was talking at once. In the blur, I heard words like "sprain" and "twisted" and "broken."

I heard Alex say she couldn't get up or stand or put any weight on her foot.

"What happened?" I asked, squeezing through the crowd.

"Didn't you see? Everybody else in the whole world did."

"I know. But how?"

"*Somebody* painted A. R. LOVES S. H. in a big red heart on Dad's volcano. I saw it right before the show, so I got some of the stage crew to help me turn it around a little. But I forgot that the corner was sticking out, and I fell."

I knew she was going to say the play was ruined. I knew she was going to say it was all my fault.

"I didn't do it!" I said.

"We know, honey." Dad pulled Joey over close to him. He must have known she painted those initials on the volcano.

Alex didn't get mad. She didn't say it was all my fault or Joey's. She started to cry. "I worked so hard for this, and now—"

"Maybe you can still go out there," I said.

"Yeah, right! I can't even stand up."

Alex looked so pathetic. I wished there was something I could do.

Mr. Cannon was pacing back and forth with his clipboard. "Think, people. We have to think. What are we going to do? We still have Act Three to go. It's short, but it's the most important act. The grand finale."

"Alex, are you sure you can't go out there?" somebody asked.

"I don't know . . ."

"You have to tell us now if you really can't go out there, honey," said Dad. "We've only got a few minutes."

"She's not going anywhere," said Mom, "but the hospital. We've got to get that foot checked."

"Mom, please. I'll be OK. Just till after the play. It's almost over. C'mon, you guys. It's *opening night.*" She said it like it was her wedding or something.

154

"Couldn't we just wrap her foot up or something, so she can walk?" I asked.

"There might be a fracture," said Mom. "It's already swollen. We can't let her put any pressure on it. She has to prop up her foot and keep that thing iced."

"OK, Alex," said Mr. Cannon. "If you can't, you can't. I don't want you to hurt yourself more than you already have. We'll think of something."

I was trying my best to think of a way to be helpful. "Don't you have an understudy?" I asked. "Somebody who knows all the lines and could take Alex's place? Act Three's really short. There are hardly any words!"

"Nina. She's the understudy," said Mr. Cannon. "But she's sick tonight. Maybe we can just go out and explain to folks what happened."

"It's opening night!" said Alex. "You can't just tell everybody to go home. People will be mad. And want their money back or something. If I know anything about acting, it's that you don't quit. You keep going, no matter what!"

"But nobody knows the lines," said Mr. Cannon.

"'I see before me a prince, more beautiful than Love itself,'" I couldn't help quoting, even though my voice was shaking. "'But where is my Beast? What has become of him?'"

"Stevie!" said Alex. "That's it! It's perfect. Hey, Mr. Cannon, my sister Stevie knows all the lines. We practiced this scene at home like a million gazillion times." She turned to me. "You mean? Really? You would do this? For me?"

I must have been crazy. Loony. Loco. I don't know what got into me. Me! The only Reel without an acting gene! As much as I wanted to help Alex, I suddenly didn't think I could go through with it.

I thought of telling Alex I'd gone nuts. Temporary insanity. I thought of saying I didn't know the lines. I thought of running out the back door.

But then I looked at my sister. She looked like a raccoon, with her stage makeup all smeary. I looked at Mom. She nodded yes. I looked at Dad. "You know what I always say. The show must go on!" Dad said.

"Where's the dressing room?" I asked.

"Act Three cast members," called Mr. Cannon, "four minutes and counting."

"Thank you—four!" everybody called back.

Including me—Beauty.

On my way to get dressed, Alex and Joey hooked pinkies with me and we did our secret handshake, "Sisters, Blisters, and Tongue Twisters."

Alex pressed a tiny gold star on a chain into my hand.

"What's this?" I asked.

"It's from my baby bracelet. I always wear it. Put it on."

Since good luck was bad luck in acting, I asked, "For bad luck?"

"Yes! Now go!" Alex whispered. Joey added a little push, and before I knew it, I was on the dark stage, behind the curtain.

Guess what, everybody? The dress didn't help. The makeup didn't help. Not even the Sisters Handshake and the bad-luck charm seemed to help.

I did not feel like Beauty one bit. I felt more like the Scarecrow in *The Wizard of Oz*.

"Curtain time!"

My knees went all wobbly. I had not walked in high heels since I was four. My eyes kept sticking together from all the makeup, and my dress crackled as loud as a potato-chip bag when I walked onstage.

Return of the Human Piñata.

In my head, I could hear Alex saying, "Try not to blink so much," and Dad saying, "Remember to say your *t*'s at the ends of words" and "Walk like you have a book on your head," and Mom saying, "You'll be fine," and Joey saying, "Go kiss a Paper Towel," but I really wasn't hearing any of them.

Then the curtain went up. The room got spooky-quiet. It was so dark, I couldn't see any faces out there.

I pretended it was *King Lear*.

At home.

In my own living room.

I took three deep breaths (Dad would be proud) and walked right out onto that stage.

A single stage light shone on Beast like a moonbeam. He was lying down in the garden. I was supposed to come up to him from behind the volcano and think he was dead.

The light was so spooky and everything was so quiet, I almost believed it myself.

I stepped into the story.

"Where, oh, where, is Beast? Why hasn't he come?" I said, looking around. Then when I saw him there, like he was really dead, I threw myself down, landing on my knees, and bent over him.

He smelled funny, like Tic Tacs and old attics.

I almost lost it. I could hardly keep from cracking up. I bent down to pretend I was listening to his heartbeat.

"My dear Beet! Your heart still beasts!" I said. Oh, no! I was getting all tongue-twisty. Why did we have to say "Tongue Twisters" right before I came onstage?

I said the line again. I think I sprayed him with spit that time.

Scott Towel, from inside his hairy costume, whispered, "Water," without moving his lips, and I remembered this was the part where Beauty was supposed to go and get water from the canal.

When I came back, I threw the water in his face.

That part was fun! Way better than spit.

"Beauty! Is it indeed you? You forgot your promise! The grief I felt at losing you made me wish to die of hunger. Now I must die, but not without the pleasure of seeing you once more."

He sat up. I kept trying really hard not to think of paper towels.

"Dear Beast, you shall not die," I said. "You shall live and become my husband. Here and now I offer you my hand and swear that I shall marry none but you."

The stage went pitch-black. Scott threw off his Beast head. He unzipped his hairy costume to reveal the Prince costume underneath. Lights blinked and flashed all around us. Music blared. A trumpet sounded.

I gasped. "I see before me a prince, more beautiful than Love itself. But where is my Beast? What has become of him?"

Scott Towel explained about the wicked fairy and how she had put a spell on him, turning him into a Beast until someone agreed to love and marry him.

All of a sudden, while Scott was giving his speech, I remembered.

Help! It was coming.

The moment Alex had waited for.

The kiss!

I had forgotten all about it. I'd been so busy thinking of Alex and the one thing I could do to make her want to be my sister again.

I couldn't look at Scott Towel. I stared at the floor.

I couldn't think. I didn't know what to do. Alex would kill me if I kissed him. But she'd also kill me if I didn't.

Just pretend he's a roll of paper towels, I told myself. *Paper towels, paper towels . . .*

And before I knew it, Beast kissed me—my cheek, anyway. I turned my head to the side in the nick of time.

The audience went wild. I guess it was OK. Alex wasn't going to kill me after all.

Once I got through the kiss, the rest of the play was a blur. I was standing here, standing there, stage left, stage right, saying this, saying that. It was like I was floating. All the words came out, and I didn't throw up once. For ten minutes, I felt like a princess. And here was Beast, telling me I was to become his queen.

You know the rest—the Happily Ever After part and all that.

The curtain fell. The audience clapped for a long time. Alex used one of the play props, an old umbrella, to hobble out at the end and take a bow. She got a standing ovation, and I got to take two curtain calls with her. I know the clapping was mostly for Alex, but a part of it was for me, too.

Alex even gave me flowers. (The ones she had sent to herself!) She kept the ones Mom and Dad gave her.

Dad used to say to me, "You're a member of the Reel family. You better start *acting* like it." I know it's corny, but that's Dad.

I guess I'm a real member of the Reel family after all.

All that Glitters

Can I just say, Broken-Foot Alex is much nicer than regular Alex?

The week after the play, Alex sent Joey and me a note (not a Silent Treatment note—a real invitation, in writing, with glitter!) that said:

WHO: Stevie + Joey
WHAT: Special (not emergency!) Meeting
   of the Sisters Club
WHEN: Tonight, Friday the 10th
WHERE: Alex's room
WHY: Surprise!
Be there! BYOSB!

I guess she couldn't help bossing on that last line. But the rest of it was so cool. Especially the part that said to Bring Your Own Sleeping Bag.

"She UN-quit!" said Joey. "Alex is back in the Sisters Club!" She was spinning. That's Joey—Human Merry-Go-Round.

I had some surprises of my own in mind, too!

Dear Sock Monkey:
Finally! I get to go to a sleepover . . .
in my big sister's room! What should
I take with me?
—Head Scratcher (a.k.a. Joey)

Dear Scratcher:
Here's a list of stuff to take:
- Sleeping bag
- Favorite pillow
- Good book
- Flashlight for reading in "bed"
- PJ's
- Popcorn
- Glitter nail polish you stole from Alex(!)
- And don't forget your favorite stuffed
  animal (not 150 of them, please). May
  I suggest a . . . sock monkey!

＊ Sock Monkey ＊

Sisters, Blisters, and Tongue Twisters!

When we got to Alex's room that night, it was dark, but the ceiling shone with glow-in-the-dark stars, giving off an eerie green light. Candles, real candles, flickered all around the room. It was just like stepping into a magical scene from *The Twelve Dancing Princesses*.

"We don't have to put on another play, do we?" I asked.

"No, Princess Smarty-Pants," said Alex. "Just sister fun!"

"Yippee!" said Joey. "Are we sleeping over? For real?"

"For real," said Alex.

"A sleepover," said Joey. "Under the stars, just like

166

pioneers! Can we eat funny food and have a pillow fight and tell fortunes and scary stories and play the Remembering Game and stuff?"

"Whatever you want, Duck. This is your night. *Our* night. Just us sisters."

First Alex gave us each a pillowcase with our name on it, so we could each have our own pillow for the pillow fight.

"You actually sewed this yourself, as in embroidered?" I asked.

"Who knew?" said Alex.

"Wow!" said Joey. "This is good. My favorite color, too."

"All colors are your favorite, Duck," I told her, and we cracked up.

"Well, Mom showed me the stitches," said Alex. "Taping her show isn't taking up as much time now that she's getting used to it."

"Mom?" I asked.

"Mom?" Joey repeated.

"Our Mom? The one who stirs her coffee with a pencil?" I asked.

"And makes spaghetti in a blender?" Joey added.

"Just 'cause she can't cook doesn't mean she can't do other stuff like sew. Don't forget she made your pioneer dress, Joey."

"OK. I have something, too," I said, handing her a box. "From Joey and me. And Dad, too, sort of. I hope you like it."

Alex opened the box. Inside was a new fuzzy blue sweater, but instead of a star in the middle, it had a peace sign.

"It's almost just like my lucky sweater! I LOVE it." Alex put it on over her pj's.

"Are you sure? 'Cause I couldn't find the one with the star."

"It's really cool. Thanks, you guys!"

"Dad helped us!" said Joey.

"Really?" asked Alex. "Dad hates the mall."

"He said it wouldn't kill him to see how the other half lives—whatever that means," said Joey.

"Whatever you do, don't cut the tag out," I told her. "And DO NOT let me wash it. Ever. Unless you like that spaghetti-in-a-blender look."

We played Blink and Spit and Steal the Pile and, best of all, the Remembering Game. Joey remembered the Macaroni Disaster, I remembered Suds-O-Rama, and Alex remembered when I was Beauty in the play. It made me feel good that she knew how hard it was for me to get up there in front of the whole entire world.

I think it was her way of thanking me.

We painted each other's toenails with glitter nail polish. (Alex actually let us use her stuff without doing a Sherlock Holmes on us!) I took a picture of our three pairs of feet, something to remember this night by.

Then we ate blue cupcakes (I stole one of Alex's magazines for the recipe) and mini bunny slippers I made out of marshmallows, frosting, and sprinkles.

"These are yum!" said Joey.

"I'm not eating mine," said Alex. "Too cute. You could sell these—you should go into business."

For dessert, we toasted marshmallows by candle-light.

Joey took out a fondue fork, put three marsh-mallows on it, and held it up to the candle. "Just like camp!" said Joey. "And this is the campfire."

"This is great! How'd you ever think of this?" I asked Alex.

"I read it in a magazine," she said. "What else?"

"What, like the *Marshmallow Times*?" I asked.

"Kidding!" she said. And we all died laughing, remembering Marshmallow Toes.

"If this is the campfire, we have to have a spooky story," said Joey.

"Three Sisters!" Joey and I yelled at the same time. "The Three Sisters" is our favorite story. Alex tells it the best, because she always changes it around to keep us guessing.

"C'mon, Alex! Tell it! Tell it!" Joey said. And I took up the chant. "Tell it! Tell it! Tell it!"

"OK, OK. You don't have to get so hyper. I'll tell it."

FULL LONG-NIGHT MOON
Starring Alex

Me: Once a long time ago there were three
sisters—

Joey: Just like us?

Me: Just like us. All three sisters were
going to be married.

Joey: Even me?

Me: Even you, Duck. OK, so the story goes,
one dark night they arrived at the inn
where they were each to meet their
true loves, who were to have come down
out of the mountains that day. But
something happened—something terrible.
Nobody showed up.

Joey: Nobody?

Stevie: Not even one out of three?

Me: Shhh. Listen. Nobody showed up, and the
three sisters were brokenhearted. They
wept all night. One was certain her love
had been killed in a blinding snowstorm.
Another thought hers had drowned in a

mountain lake, and the third was convinced
that her love was buried in an avalanche
way up high at the snow line.

They wept and wept until . . . the next
day. Finally, they hiked to the foot of
the mountain. They made a crude headstone
out of wood, and each sister decided to
carve the name of her true love in it
to mark the place of his death.

The oldest sister went first.

Stevie: Of course!

Me: The oldest sister carved the name of
her true love. When the other two sisters
saw the name, they went faint. Each of
their true loves was one and the same!

Joey: They all loved the same guy?

Me: Yes, but he had disappeared. They never,
ever saw him again.

Stevie: What a creep.

Me: Don't you mean what a stinkard?

Stevie: A pox on him for sure!

Joey: What happened then?

Me: Years later, after the sisters died, there

was a terrible earthquake, which split
the mountain into four mountains.
To this very day, they call the mountains
the Three Sisters.

Joey: You said four.

Me: Three are together. One is off in the
distance—Mount Bachelor. But nobody could
live near the Three Sisters.

Joey: Why not?

Me: The mountains are volcanoes. Every two
thousand years they erupt, because the
sisters were so angry at the guy.

Joey: Why couldn't they live there the rest
of the time?

Me: Oh. Well, because of the moaning. *Oooooo,
Aaahhhhhh.* The chilling sound could
always be heard whistling and moaning
through the mountain passes, and
it haunted the people of the village of
Acton below. Some said it was just the
wind. Others were certain it was the three
sisters, moaning for their lost love.

Joey: Really?

Me: Some got so frightened, they moved away.
But no matter how many villagers came
and went, the Three Sisters stayed together,
forever, for the rest of time.

Joey: You gave me shivers.

Stevie: Me, too.

Me: So be it. That is the Legend of the Three
Sisters. Just look out the window.

*(The three sisters climb on Alex's bed and
kneel, looking out the window.)*

Stevie: There's a full moon. Hey, I think I
can see the Three Sisters!

Joey: Listen. I think I hear something, like
moaning.

Stevie: That's a cat.

Me: Look at all the shadows. I love full-moon
nights. It makes you feel all different and
quivery.

Stevie: I know.

Me: Did you know all the full moons have
names? Like Moon of Falling Leaves and

Wolf Moon and stuff? Tonight is called the Full Long-Night Moon.

Stevie: That's cool. Did you read *that* in a magazine?

Me: No. A calendar.

Joey: Let's make this the longest night ever.

Stevie: Duck, it's way past your bedtime. You can hardly keep your eyes open now.

Me: Before we go to sleep, we have one more thing to do.

Joey: What?

Me: Make a wish.

Native American Names for Moons

January • Wolf Moon *Scott "Howl" Moon?*

February • Snow Moon *Cool!*

March • Maple Sugar Moon *Yum!*

April • Frog Moon, Pink Moon

May • Milk Moon, Flower Moon

June • Strawberry Moon *→ fondue*

July • Thunder Moon

August • Moon of the Green Corn

September • Harvest Moon

October • Moon of Falling Leaves

November • Frost Moon, Beaver Moon

December • Full Long-Night Moon *My favorite!*

Make a Wish

Alex reached over and pulled something out from under her bed. It looked like a tiny stack of origami paper tied with a red bow.

"What is it?" asked Joey.

"Wishing paper," said Alex.

The paper was so wispy-thin, you could almost see through it. On the front were gold and birds and red stamps of Chinese characters.

"We each get one," said Alex. "You write down your wishes, then throw them into the fire. We can take turns burning our wishing papers in the candle."

"Did you ask Mom if we're allowed to do this?" I asked.

"Yes, but we have to do it over a cookie sheet. I promised."

"Do we have to say 'Sisters, Blisters, and Tongue Twisters'?" Joey asked.

"Yep. Good idea, Duck. Then our wishes will go into the universe and come back true."

"Can it be a dream?" Joey asked.

"It can be a dream," Alex said.

Alex's hopes, dreams, plans for the future

* Be on Mom's show
* Get S. H. to sign my cast ♡
* Never eat another marshmallow
* Play Juliet someday
* Did I mention . . . play Juliet?

Stevie's dreams (and schemes!)

~ World Peace (family peace, too)
~ My own room
~ Publish a poem
~ Start my own business
~ Always have the Sisters Club

JOEY'S WISHES

• A million dollars
• Go to Pioneer Camp
• A baby sister (someone to boss!)
• Hold a monkey (not a sock one)
• Never, EVER be kissed by a boy

After we sent our wishes out into the universe, Joey and I helped Alex blow out all the candles. I curled up into my sleeping bag, with my new Stevie pillowcase on my pillow. The room smelled all cinnamon-y, like it remembered the burning of candles.

Before I fell asleep, I thought about my tiny wishes, floating out there in the wide, wide universe, under the Full Long-Night Moon. I imagined my wishes floating right next to Alex's and Joey's, high up as a star. Maybe our wishes would make their own constellation, one that kids would point to on summer nights, saying, "Hey, isn't that the Three Sisters?"

"I wish I was ten," Joey said to the dark.

"You're not supposed to say what you wished for!" said Alex.

"That wasn't my wish for the universe. I just thought of it right now."

"How come ten?" Alex asked.

"'Cause ten's the BEST age," I said.

"In *The Long Winter*, Laura Ingalls Wilder says—" Joey began.

"Here we go," I said.

"You read *The Long Winter*?" asked Alex. "*The Long*

Winter is like the longest book in the world. Even I never finished it."

"Longer than Dad's all-time favorite, *War and Peace*?" I asked.

"In *The Long Winter,* it says Baby Carrie was not really a sister until she was ten. When she turned ten, Laura said she was old enough to really be a sister."

"Go to sleep, Joey," said Alex.

"You're really a sister," I whispered to Joey before we fell asleep.

The only sounds now were the heartbeat tick of the clock, the hum and creak of house noises, and Alex breathing.

I lay on the rug between my sisters, Alex on one side, Joey on the other, like perfect bookends. I couldn't think of anywhere I'd rather be.

In the middle.

MEGAN McDONALD

is the author of the immensely popular
Judy Moody series and its companion
series starring Judy's brother, Stink.
She is also the author of *Ant and Honey
Bee,* a picture book illustrated by Brian
Karas. The youngest of five sisters,
Megan McDonald lives in Sebastopol,
California.